Welcome to Country Acres

Tales From Country Acres
Book One: *Heirs of the Dirt*

ISBN: 979-8-9953843-1-1

Published by
Grand Media Publishing

TALES FROM COUNTRY ACRES
HEIRS OF THE DIRT

CREATED & WRITTEN BY
JAMES Q. LEACH

Grand Media Publishing

CHAPTER ONE
Summer Friends, Summer Not

A weather-beaten sign stood alone where the pavement gave up, announcing in peeling paint *Welcome to Country Acres.*

The further Mrs. Lila Mae Berry's car rumbled down the winding backroads, the more the air seemed to change. Notes of wild honeysuckle slipped through the rolled-down windows, mixing with pine and the damp, rich scent of the earth. Sunlight flashed through the windshield in uneven bursts, as if the country were introducing itself the only way it knew how.

The little boy in the backseat took it all in, unaware that some places don't loosen their grip once they've laid eyes on you.

When the car finally stopped, he clutched the handle of his small blue suitcase and dragged it behind him as he climbed out.

There were no sidewalks.

No skyscrapers.

No traffic jams.

No buzzing city hum.

Just dirt roads, fruit trees, the distant gurgle of a creek nearby, and the chirping of a thousand unseen cicadas.

His stomach tightened with a mix of excitement and nerves.

Mrs. Lila Mae stood with her hands planted on her hips, watching him wobble up the steps and learn the feel of the uneven boards beneath his feet.

"Michael, sweetie, you's gon' have a good summer here," she said.

Her voice was firm and warm, carrying authority that left no room for debate.

"Now don't just stand there. Go put your bags up in the room and come back out. I want you to meet somebody."

After stashing his bags, he wandered back to the front yard where she smiled and nodded toward the field.

"C'mon. Let's go now," she said, nudging his small shoulders.

He followed her across an open stretch of land toward a cluster of houses waiting on the other side.

That's when Mike met Quan Richards.

Country Acres called him Q.

Already, the boy was a blur of motion, firing a baseball against the side of a barn and calling his own strikes. His face smeared with dirt and sunlight, bare feet kicking up dust with every move. When he turned and locked eyes with Mike, he waved like he was greeting someone he'd been waiting on.

"Mornin' Mrs. Lila Mae," Q casually called out, as if he spoke to her every day.

That's because he did.

"You the really smart grandboy Mrs. Lila Mae been talkin' about?" he said, squinting like he was sizing him up for a challenge.

"Yes, my name's Mike," he responded.

A horse nearby let out a loud, sudden neigh.

Mike shuffled back a step, unsure what to do.

"Don't worry 'bout that, Cityboy. You'll get used to it," Q said, already grinning.

He scooped up a basketball he had nearby and sent it right toward Mike's chest.

Just like the new nickname, Mike caught it.

"Good catch," Q said, giving a small, confident nod.

Mike felt a little less like an outsider.

Quick as that, the introductions were done. Mrs. Lila Mae headed back, and Mike was on his own.

***

The boys spent the afternoon playing sports, roaming the woods, racing down country slopes, and daring each other to cross the creek on wet, wobbly logs that served as bridges.

Mike didn't want the day to end. Everything about it felt bigger, brighter, louder than anything he'd known before.

"Wanna meet my best friend?" Q asked, a sly grin tugging at his dirt-smudged face.

He led Mike to the far corner of the yard, where a sagging fence leaned like it was guarding secrets. The chain rattled as he pulled it open, revealing a shadow crouched low in the dirt.

"This here's Bullet," he announced, pride in his voice, almost daring Mike to question it.

Mike raised an eyebrow. "The dog named Bullet?"

"Cause he really-really fast," Q replied, firm, like the matter was settled.

A scrappy German Shepherd stepped out from the doghouse, ribs showing beneath his coat. His eyes stayed locked on Q, never drifting to Mike.

There was no mistaking it.

The dog's whole world revolved around that boy.

"I don't believe that," Mike said, grinning like he was calling Q's bluff. "He does not look fast. Let him out. I want to see."

For half a second, Q hesitated.

His hand hovered over the gate latch, pride and caution wrestling in his chest.

"Ain't posed to let him out when momma at work," he said, his voice thinner.

But in the country, taunts are heavier than rules. He felt his chest swell with the need to prove something.

Mike waited to see what he would do.

Q snapped the latch. The gate creaked wide open.

Bullet exploded like a cork from a bottle, slamming Q into the dirt. His tail whipped side to side in excitement. His tongue covered Q's face like he'd been caged a lifetime. Q laughed, winded, trying to push him back.

"Hold on, Bullet, I gotta get your leash!"

A rabbit darted across the yard.

Bullet locked on.

His ears stood at attention. Muscles tightened.

Then he was gone.

"BULLET! GET BACK HERE!" Q screamed, panic cracking through each syllable.

The dog didn't hear Q, or he just didn't care. He never looked back.

He cleared the fence line and hit the dirt road just as Old Man Willy's tractor rattled down the lane.

The thump came quick.

Cruel.

Final.

The road seemed to hold its breath for a split second. Dust hung in the air.

Bullet lay still in the road.

Old Man Willy climbed down, his face pale beneath his sweat-stained hat. His voice was low, cracked like old barn wood. "Lord help me... Q, I-I ain't see him, son."

Q dropped to his knees, hands hovering over Bullet, whispering frantic words he barely understood.

Mike stood a few feet away, frozen, watching for what felt like hours. He took a careful step closer and placed a hand gently on Q's back.

"He might be okay, Q," Mike said, mostly to convince himself.

Q's chest heaved. Sobs tore out raw.

"It's my fault," he choked, rocking back and forth, hands buried in the dog's scruff.

Mike's stomach twisted, shame burning deep in his gut.

In the city, words disappeared into noise.

Out here, they stayed.

His own sharp, careless words from earlier cut deeper now. He crouched low beside Q. "No, it's not just you. I pushed you to let him out."

The two boys sat in the road, grief hanging heavy in the summer heat.

Q wiped his tears, voice barely steady.

"We both stupid."

For the first time in their lives, Q and Mike felt what friendship really cost. In that quiet, invisible moment, something entered between them—trust, care, and the unspoken start of a bond that could last a lifetime.

They didn't leave Bullet in the road.

Loyalty and honor came first.

Leaving him there would have been another kind of wrong.

Together, hands too small for such a heavy chore, they took an old shovel and dug a shallow grave beneath an aged pecan tree that leaned over the creek.

Q pressed a flat rock at the head, scratching *BULLET* into its face with a rusty nail. Mike carved the name again into the tree bark above, leaving a rough scar the tree would carry for years.

When it was done, the boys lay side by side in the grass, shoes kicked off, faces streaked with dust and sweat. The sun dipped low, painting the sky with streaks of fire.

Q finally spoke, not looking at Mike, not looking at the grave.

"I ain't ever buried nothin' before," he said. His voice was rough, like it didn't belong to him. "Didn't think it'd feel like this."

Mike swallowed hard, the sting of guilt still sharp. He turned his head toward Q.

"I'm sorry," he said. "I didn't mean for none of this to happen."

Q nodded once.

Just once.

"I know," he said.

But the way he said it meant he would remember it anyway.

Mike nodded, watching the fireflies start their slow, flickering dance.

He felt a strange pull toward Country Acres, a belonging the northern city life had never given him. And for the first time, he didn't mind leaving it all behind, even if it was just for two months to visit his grandmother.

In the orchard, the trees swayed, leaning in as if to watch Q and Mike's friendship grow alongside the land.

As the last sun streaks faded, Mike rolled over on the grass and sighed.

"I have to go, Q. Grandma might fuss at me if I'm late for dinner." He brushed dirt from his elbows and gave Q a faint, lopsided grin. "Think we can play again tomorrow?"

Q sat up, hugging his knees. His face was still puffy from crying, but a flicker of relief shined through his eyes.

"Yeah," he said simply. "Tomorrow."

Mrs. Lila Mae's voice carried from the porch, sharp but warm, calling across the yard.

"Miiichael, time to come home and get supper!"

She squinted against the sinking sun, hands braced on her hips. From where she stood, she saw two boys stretched out in the grass by the creek, unaware the spot was now a gravesite marked by stone and scarred bark.

Her voice softened to herself, "Them's the boys this land needs."

She didn't know what storms might come, but in her heart she hoped the bond would root deep, strong enough to carry the land forward when she no longer could.

The creek gurgled softly nearby, as if the land itself had been listening.

Mike kicked his shoes back on and started toward the porch, the boards creaking under his weight as he climbed the steps.

Halfway up, he turned back.

Q was still sitting in the grass by the grave, shoulders rounded, eyes fixed on the tree they'd carved. He didn't look like the same boy who had been so happy that morning.

Something heavier had settled over him.

A weight he would carry forever.

Mike swallowed hard, then followed the smell of supper inside, the screen door slapping shut behind him.

CHAPTER TWO
Throw Some Dirt On It

The sun rose on burnt grass and stretches of dirt yards.

Q was already out, picking up sticks and tossing them in a pile, as if the day itself were a game he meant to win. He spotted Mike walking toward him, kicking up red puffs of dust with each step.

The boys had barely exchanged their hellos.

A flash of movement caught Mike's eyes.

A vibrant little girl skipped along the far side of the dirt road, ribbon bows and beads bouncing in her neatly braided hair.

Mike froze.

She was the prettiest girl he had ever seen. Her cheeks shined as she pushed out a bright smile. His stomach clenched with a feeling he didn't yet have words for.

Country folk call it puppy love.

"Hey, Q! You wanna come over and jump on the trampoline today?" she called.

"Yeah, we'll come by later. We fixin' to head down to the lake," he yelled back.

"Who's that?" Mike whispered, trying to sound casual. His goofy little grin betrayed him, full of boyish wonder.

"That's Red," Q said, like it was nothing.

"Her real name's Candace. We go to the same school."

He shrugged like that explained everything. He smirked as he caught the way Mike's eyes lingered.

"You like her, don't you."

"No," a lie Mike shot back too fast. His face told the truth plain as day.

Red came skipping out of the brush, the beads in her hair clinking.

"I'm comin' too," she called out. "Bet I catch mo' fish this time."

Q brushed it off. "You wish."

Red stopped short and looked Mike up and down. "Who you?"

The boy froze stiff.

Q scratched at his neck. "This here Mike. Mrs. Lila Mae's grandboy, all way from up 'nawf."

"Baltimore," Mike finally chimed in, puffing a little with pride. "Maryland."

"Murrrland," Red repeated, stretching it out a twang.

A slight giggle slipped through her smile.

She was obviously teasing, the kind that implied she liked the sound of it.

Mike grinned, bashful, knowing he liked the way she said it better.

Q caught it quick as a snakebite.

He cut in, "Headed to the creek," already stompin' off with a stick in his hand, daring them to keep up.

The trio made their way to the end of the creek, where it met the lake.

Junction Lake.

The creek's chatter faded there. The water spread wide and quiet, like it was keeping something to itself.

Mike was being careful on the stones, Red was stepping all around them.

If you didn't know Q, you might've thought he was trying to show off.

He naturally jumped over the logs.

Took off running without warning.

Chased things that only he could see.

Swung sticks like magic wands, slinging creek water in wild arcs.

The ruler of his own make-believe world.

Every move was quick and deliberate, shaped by a life spent in dirt and trees.

He glanced back.

Red and Mike had peeled off, settling on the old splintery dock that leaned a few feet into the lake like it might give up any second. Their bare feet dangled, toes brushing the water. Mike said something low that made Red laugh and swat his arm, but she didn't pull her hand away right off. He leaned closer. She didn't lean back.

Q felt it before he understood it.

Something tight. Something hot.

Not anger. Not hurt. Just a sting.

Jealousy didn't feel right.

He caught the look in Red's eyes and the way Mike didn't notice him watching.

Q bit the inside of his lip and turned away with a short smirk that didn't quite land.

If they wanted to sit and whisper, fine.

He'd give them something to look at.

Out on the lake, a half-rotten log floated just beneath the surface, slick with moss, darkened by murky water.

Q hopped onto it easily, balancing like he'd done it a hundred times before. He didn't look back to see if they were watching.

He walked across it, hopping once, then twice, testing it the way boys who grew up near water learn to do.

Mike and Red watched from the dock.

Red shouted out, "Good landin' Q."

She saw it.

Her and Mike both followed him with an interest that didn't bother hiding.

That's when it happened.

Mike puffed his chest up.

He stood up like he belonged there too.

He jumped from the dock, trying to land on the log.

Wrong move.

The moment his foot hit the log, it shifted.

There was a sharp crack, hollow and wrong, and the wood split right under his feet.

Mike dropped straight into the lake.

Cold water swallowed him whole.

He came up sputtering, eyes wide with panic and terror. "I can't—I can't swim!" he cried, then was taken under again.

The world went silent inside of Q.

For a moment, everything vanished.

Nothing mattered.

There was only Mike.

Flailing in water.

Drowning.

Q didn't think. He didn't have time to.

He dove in hard, water slapping his chest as he reached Mike, just as panic pulled him down. He wrapped an arm across Mike's chest and kicked, fighting the drag of the water, hauling him back toward the bank.

His feet scraped the bottom.

Then rock.

Then dirt.

He shoved Mike up onto the edge.

Mike coughed and cried, sucking in air like it was the first breath he'd ever taken.

Red gasped from the dock, her hands flying to her mouth. Her eyes stayed locked on the boys.

She wasn't laughing.

She wasn't teasing.

She was just watching.

There was something quiet and new settling over her—awe and respect.

Q climbed out the water, chest heaving. He didn't look at Red. He didn't look at Mike. He just stayed there, wringing lake water from his shirt.

He stayed quiet longer than usual.

Water still dripping from his sleeves, his focus stayed on the lake. Not the boy he'd just pulled out of it.

For a moment, he felt smaller somehow.

Then he turned back.

"Can't be doin' stuff like that, you dummy," Q shouted, his tone harsher now. "That could've killed you."

Mike deflated.

Q glanced toward the dark stretch of water. "It'll take your life if you ain't careful."

Mike swallowed, rubbing his arm. "I wasn't trying to be dumb," he said, his voice wobbling just a little. "I was just trying to be like you."

That landed harder than the fall.

Q turned away. He sealed his mouth and stared at the mud between his bare feet.

"Shouldn't jump in water if you can't swim," he said, words edged with venom. Then, softer, "I knew I shouldn't have brought you out here."

Red finally found her voice. "He ain't wrong, Mike" she said, arms crossed, still shaken. "This lake took a kid last summer. Folk still don't talk about it."

Q's head dropped. His eyes stayed on the water a second too long.

Mike hissed, lifting his foot. A thin red line cut across the bottom.

"I think I need a band-aid," he said.

Q looked at Mike's foot. Then at Red.

They both traded the same look, half annoyed, half amused.

Then, as if they'd practiced it, they spoke at the same time.

"Throw some dirt on it."

***

The sun was high and unforgiving.

It didn't take long for their clothes to dry, the heat baking the fear right out of them until the lake felt farther away than it was.

By the time they ended up in the grass beneath some apple trees, the moment had settled into something quieter. The kind of quiet that comes after you almost lose something.

All three of them collapsed on the grass, eating fresh apples. Q's hands were dirt-streaked, knees scraped, but he forced himself to look casual.

Red broke the silence first.

"Ain't nobody need to hear 'bout this," she said, eyes sharp.

Q agreed.

She continued, "We tell our folks, they ain't gon' let us come back outside 'til school start."

Mike swallowed. He knew she might be right. He nodded once and stomped his foot into the dust. "Nobody!" he said, louder than he meant to.

The word felt heavier than it should've. It hung there, thicker than the heat, settling into the dirt between them.

Q's eyes narrowed. *That's some city stuff*, he thought. *Ain't how we do it in Country Acres.*

Q scraped the toe of his shoe through the dust, then looked out toward the trees lining the water, land stretching out around them.

He stood up quick.

"Hey Mike," he said, dusting off his hands. "Remember this here our land. Our dirt."

Mike followed Q's gaze toward the trees, the creek, and the dirt under their feet. The field felt less like a place to play and more like something they had to protect.

"I'm king of this here dirt, and don't nothin' come between that," Q continued. His voice low, almost a growl. "No money. No power. No nothin'."

Mike raised an eyebrow. "What do you mean by that?"

Q glanced at Mike, sizing him up. "You might be a visitor, but today, you can be an honorary king, too," he said.

He dug a tiny nick in his thumb with a nail from the fence post and pressed his bloody finger into the dirt in front of them. "Promise me," he said, "Right here. Blood in the dirt. Say it: No Money. No Power. No Nothin'. Kings of the Dirt."

Mike winced. He glanced at Red, who was waiting to see what he would do, then pricked his own thumb and stuck it in the dirt next to Q's.

A small bead of blood seeped into the dry earth.

"Kings of the dirt," he said softly, knowing he had just agreed to something he didn't fully understand.

Red leaned back on a tree, curious but left out. The boys didn't invite her in. The oath wasn't hers to join. A trace of disappointment crossed her face before she buried it.

By the time the sun dipped low, the three children were walking home. Red walked a step ahead, pointing across the fence line toward a small cluster of cows.

"That one's Daisy. And that one there's Sheba," she said matter-of-factly, like it was something everyone ought to know.

Mike listened, smiling, trying to remember the names.

Q trailed a few steps back, staring hard at the soil beneath the apple trees, where blood had been pressed into the dirt. The land had already taken it in, dark and quiet.

He felt something settle in his chest, heavy and unfamiliar.

Some things didn't wash out. They stayed.

The cicadas kept singing, like nothing had happened at all.

CHAPTER THREE
Summer Came. Summer Went.

Summer didn't end all at once. It stretched, settled, and rooted itself into long days that blurred together.

Q, Mike, and Red were rarely apart.

On hot afternoons, they would lose hours at the arcade on Main Street, feeding quarters into machines until Mrs. Lila Mae came looking for them herself. If one showed up, the other two weren't far behind.

By the time weeks had passed, the land barely remembered them as strangers. The days no longer felt numbered. Two months had passed by.

Red usually sat on the porch rail this time of day, swinging her legs and naming things she knew, but the rail was empty.

Mike sat on the porch steps with his elbows on his knees, suitcase leaning against the post. His sneakers were scuffed with red dirt, and his T-shirt smelled faintly of creek water and smoke from the previous night's bonfire.

The car was already packed. His mother was inside talking with Grandma Lila Mae, but Mike wasn't ready to let summer end.

Q came trudging up from the back side of the barnyard, a stick swinging at his side. He squatted in the grass across from Mike, eyes steady, no smile this time.

"You look like you headed to war," Q said, nudging the suitcase with his stick.

"Feels like it," Mike said under his breath. He gave a half-grin as the sunlight caught it. "Man, Q, this was the best summer ever."

Q shrugged, though his chest tightened. "Yeah, it was alright, I guess."

Mike leaned back, eyes drifting out over the apple orchard and the shimmer of the creek in the distance. "No, it wasn't just alright. We caught all of them fish down at the river, remember? I caught that catfish that was bigger than your arm."

"I had to help you reel him in, y'almost lost him," Q corrected him, smirking now.

"Yes, but I baited the hook."

"You lost the first four worms."

They went back and forth until they both broke out in laughter, voices bouncing off the porch rails. Then it faded. The quiet that followed felt different. Like something was counting down.

Mike filled it with more memories.

"And the trail rides. Man, those ribs off the food truck was delicious. And the funnel cakes. I thought I was going to pass out."

"You did pass out," Q said. "Soon as we got home, you was stretched out on the couch with that white sugar powder on your chin."

Mike chuckled. "City food does not taste like that, Q. Nothing in Baltimore does."

The smile stayed, but something heavier landed in his eyes. His voice softened, "I really don't want to leave. But summer's over, right?"

Q's stick tapped against the dirt. Once. Then again.

Kids left the country all the time. His cousins did. His neighbors did. Most of 'em didn't come back.

He'd learned not to put much faith in promises.

Mike leaned forward, trying again.

"I'm serious, Q. I'm going to come back next summer. Then, every summer. Until we're grown men and I can live here forever. Maybe even fix this place up real nice."

He paused, then said it like it mattered. "We got to keep the land safe. Nobody's taking it from us. We are the Kings of the dirt."

Q studied him, the way kids do when they don't want to show that they're scared.

"You sayin' that now, Cityboy. You'll forget once you back in ... what's it called?"

"Baltimore, Maryland," Mike said, puffing his chest.

"'Murraland,'" Q teased, slipping into Red's voice.

They both cracked up, laughter breaking the moment wide open. But when it faded, the quiet crept back in and sat heavy between them, again.

Inside the house, voices had been going for a long while. Mike could not make out the words, just the rise and fall of them.

Grandma Lila Mae's voice came slow and pleading, like she was laying something down carefully, asking for more time. Asking for space. Saying the boy was rooted here now, even if he didn't know it yet.

Mike's mother answered firmer. Sharper. Baltimore was where his life was. Where school waited. Where things were already decided. She said keeping him here would only make it harder later. Said things were changing back home, and she needed him with her.

The porch went quiet again.

Then the front door flew open.

"Mike, honey," Grandma Lila Mae called, her voice tight around the edges. "Your mama's ready."

Mike's mother came out right behind her, keys already in hand, eyes fixed on the car.

The door slammed.

The engine turned.

Mike shot to his feet, heart racing. "Dang, it's really time." He looked at Q, panic and sadness tangled together, "Summer came. Summer went."

"Uncle Ant always say the time and the world gone move, even when we don't," Q said, repeating something he'd heard his Uncle Anthony say a hundred times.

Mike reached out a hand. Awkward. Firm.

Q shook it, their grips locked for a second too long.

Then, without thinking, they hugged. A quick, solid wrap of arms. Both pulled away fast, before it got too heavy.

At the car, Mike tossed his suitcase into the backseat and climbed in. As it rolled forward, he pressed his face to the window. "I'll be back, Q!" he shouted. "I promise!"

In the driver's seat, his mother tightened her grip on the wheel. She didn't look back. Her eyes stayed fixed ahead, as if hearing him might change her mind. The car kept moving.

Q lifted his stick in the air like a salute. He didn't shout back. Didn't wave. He just stood there, watching the dust rise as the car carried Mike away. Birds and crickets filled the quiet. He watched the dust swirl where the car had been, a quiet ache settling in his chest.

He twirled the stick once, then planted it in the dirt, shoulders squared. For him, it was another goodbye. A promise he wasn't sure this land would ever let the world keep.

For Mike, it had been the best summer of his life.

The dust from the road hadn't settled when another car appeared.

Not a truck. Not a neighbor's rusted sedan. A clean, pale-colored car that moved slow, like it didn't want to startle the place.

It rolled to a stop near the edge of the fence.

A woman stepped out. Her shoes sank into the dirt just a little, and she looked down at them like the ground had done something wrong.

"Mrs. Berry?" she called, voice smooth and careful.

Mrs. Lila Mae straightened. "That'll be me."

The woman smiled and walked closer, stopping short of the porch. She held a clipboard instead of a purse.

"My name's Marsha Cross. I work with a development group out of the state office that's been surveying land in this area. We help families keep up with rising taxes and repairs, the things that come with owning something valuable. Your creek line and orchard sit on one of the last undeveloped parcels in the district."

She then gestured back toward the road, casually.
"You probably remember Mr. Henson's little barbershop. Henson's Cuts. Cars lined up on Fridays, all the way down the block."

She smiled, like it was a fond memory.

"Taxes went up. Roof needed work. He sold. Magnolia helped him relocate closer in the city."

Mrs. Lila Mae didn't return the smile. "Is that what happened, he relocated?" she smugly asked.

Q pictured the boarded building at the bend in the road, the one with the faded pole still painted on the glass. He'd never been inside. He just knew it used to be loud. Used to be full.

Cross set her clipboard against her hip. "Progress looks different depending on where you're standing."

Mrs. Lila Mae's eyes narrowed, just a touch.

"My family been owning this land my whole life," she said. "Seems to be holding up fine."

Cross nodded, like that was the answer she expected.

"Most beautiful things do," she said. "Until the world around them changes."

Q stood a few steps back, stick still in his hand. He didn't like the way the woman looked past them, not at them, but through them, her eyes drawn to the orchard and the creek line.

He figured she was just another grown-up trying to tell Mrs. Lila Mae how to run things.

Mrs. Lila Mae stepped forward, putting herself between the porch and the land.

"I'm not interested in whatever it is you's selling," she said.

Cross's smile stayed, but it softened, like she was talking to a child instead of a grown woman.

"Not today," she said. "That's alright. Maybe... another time."

She handed a business card to Mrs. Lila Mae and turned back to her car. The engine faded down the road, leaving behind a wake of dust.

Mrs. Lila Mae didn't care about the card. She didn't even read it. She folded it once and tucked it into her apron pocket like something she didn't want the wind to see.

She leaned against the porch rail, her voice steady but softer than usual. "Q, can you come cut my grass this weekend?"

"Yes, ma'am," Q answered without hesitation. "I'll be here Saturday morning, like always."

Her eyes lingered down the road a moment longer than necessary, the place where her daughter and grandson had disappeared. Something unreadable crossed her face. Then she turned back to Q and managed to smile.

"I'll pay you double this time."

Q's chest swelled. He nodded once and took off toward his house, grinning to himself, not knowing he had just been claimed by more than a weekend job.

CHAPTER FOUR
A True Legacy

Thirty years passed.

The edges of Country Acres had softened, but the morning fog still clung low to trees and curled along the red clay road. The air smelled of wet earth, pine sap, and a faint twang of livestock from nearby pastures. Birds scattered their songs between roosters and crickets, filling the quiet.

A pristine, flashy car hummed down the lane, tires crunching loose gravel. Too clean, too new, too polished for the dirt and trees around it.

The man behind the wheel rolled down the window, letting the damp, familiar air wash over him. The lines at the corners of his eyes tightened as he scanned the countryside, already calculating what it would be worth if it were sold tomorrow.

Mike hadn't been back in decades.

As he pulled up to the church, packed with most of the town's people, a quiet ache stirred in him, something he had not felt in a long time.

At the church, the townspeople had already begun gathering. Mike hesitated, gripping the doorframe of the car, feeling the weight of years stretched between him and the town he once knew.

Q was there.

He was helping older residents from their cars to the building, still careful and deliberate. His broad shoulders caught in the morning sun, dark slacks pressed clean though a hint of grit clung to the hem, as if the land itself refused to let him go completely.

He looked the same as the boy Mike had last seen, just heavier. Grounded by responsibility, by promises kept, by a lifetime spent protecting the dirt they had once claimed as theirs. It showed in the way he stood, solid and unmoving.

When he noticed Mike, he stopped for a moment.

Mike stepped from the car, heart pounding, but Q was already moving away, eyes cautious.

Q didn't wave.

He didn't even speak.

In that pause, the space of thirty summers stood between the two men, the silence louder than any words could have been.

The funeral was being held in a chapel behind the church in a low, whitewashed building whose paint peeled like old paper, exposing the wood beneath.

Inside, the air was thick with incense and the faint scent of wilted flowers placed on the altar the night before. Sunlight made its way through the stained-glass windows, casting fractured beams of deep red and gold across the pews.

Mike's city-trained eyes scanned every detail.

The polished wood under his hands. The creak of the floorboards as mourners shifted. The uneven rhythm of breath across the room. Each small sound and color pressed against memory, pulling him back to summer's long past.

He stepped down the aisle and moved toward the casket. Folks whispered.

The polished wood gleamed under the chapel lights, almost too perfect for what it held.

Mike looked down at his grandmother's face, softer now than he remembered, folded into a stillness that felt both familiar and distant.

He waited for something to rise in his chest. A rush. A crack. A release.

It didn't come.

So he stood there a moment longer anyway, fingers resting against the edge of the casket, offering the silence what he couldn't seem to find in himself. Then he stepped back, carrying the weight of a love he knew was real, even if it didn't know how to show itself.

He took his seat.

Even in a room full of grief, Country Acres had a way of announcing its own.

Red walked in and stood near the front, her posture sharp and her gaze steady. Her hair was pulled back into a simple bun of braids, a grown woman's echo of the girl he once knew. Her eyes met Mike's for the briefest moment, a spark of recognition warming his chest. But the distance of years and choices made kept a quiet wall between them.

"Good morning, Mr. Dawson. Mrs. Minnie. Mr. Whitmire," Red greeted each of the elders by name, her voice strong and confident. Subtle nods. A warm smile.

She moved among them with ease, and Mike noticed how naturally they responded, as if she had always belonged in this room.

She was now a city councilwoman, respected and deliberate in every movement. Beneath her composed exterior, the slightest flicker of old familiarity lingered. She gazed at the body, and a single tear traced down her cheek before she kept moving.

Mike noticed how the mourners smiled when they saw his grandmother. Every detail reminded him that life had pulled everyone along different paths, and that the people and land he once loved had changed in ways he could not control.

At the pulpit, the slim, neatly composed leader of the church took his rightful place.

Reverend Johnathon Brooks cleared his throat, gripping the worn wood, veins standing out like knotted roots.

"We gather here today to honor the life God lent us through our dear Mrs. Lila Mae Berry. Proverbs 13:22 says, 'A good man leaves an inheritance to his children's children'."

He continued, "Y'all, she done just that. She left more than land or buildings. She left a true legacy. She will remain in our hearts forever."

Mike shifted, letting the words sink into corners of his chest he had tried to keep quiet for years.

Q stood at the doors, arms crossed loosely, jaws tight. He didn't need the preacher to remind him of his duty. Every morning, the land had spoken to him, whispering in the wind, sighing through the trees. Mike had left, but he stayed, guarding every acre, every fencepost, every shadowed bend in the creeks. Even Mrs. Lila Mae.

The mourners continued to file in softly, shoes creaking on the wooden floor. Old men tipped their hats to Q, eyes lingering with respect.

Mike drew attention too, but his presence felt fragile, out of place in a space defined by the life and legacy of the woman they all had loved.

While neighbors murmured their sorrow, a woman in a sharp gray suit stood out among sun-faded dresses and worn work shirts.

Ms. Dana Cross.

Folks whispered her name under their breath as if it carried weight. Magnolia, INC.'s rep, the face of the company buying up half the county.

She held a neat notepad and an unreadable smile, as if even death were just another deal to watch unfold. The subtle click of her heels against the floor punctuated the quiet, like a metronome of control.

Near the side, Sheriff James Haskins stood tall and firm, uniform crisp, hands resting near his heavy belt. His eyes flicked to Dana, then away, betraying nothing, though the smallest twitch hinted at silent calculation. Together, they moved like chess players in a game the town didn't yet know they were playing.

The preacher's voice rose, steady and commanding, "Matthew 6:20 says, 'Lay up for yourselves treasures in heaven, where neither moth nor rust destroys, and where thieves do not break in and steal. Folks, Mrs. Lila Mae embodied that. She taught us to cherish what is worth keeping, and to guard it with our lives if we must. Amen to that."

The chapel held its breath.

Mike felt the weight of his grandmother's life pressing in on him. The memory of her hands, her voice, the smell of her cooking, and the creak of her porch steps wrapping around him like a soft, warm quilt. His throat tightened, and he swallowed once, steadying himself.

He turned and met Q's eyes.

Q hadn't moved, hadn't blinked. His arms stayed folded across his chest, like a gate that wasn't going to open.

No warmth. No welcome. Only the silent question: *Did he come back to honor, or to take?*

Red saw it before either of them said a word. Her glances flicked between the two. She remembered the boyhood summer. She saw it again in the space between them now.

The way Q had ruled the orchards with a stick.

Mike almost drowning in Junction Lake.

The unspoken rules and oath protecting the land.

Rules Q had lived by, and Mike had once promised to.

Decades of space had made those memories heavier, sharper. She understood Q the way few did, and she understood what was at stake now. The pull of the past, the weight of responsibility, the shadows stirring across the county, all pressed against her. She folded her hands together and stayed where she was.

Her loyalty wasn't a question. She knew which side of the land she stood on. She only hoped Mike did too. Because this time, she knew the dirt wouldn't forgive the wrong choice.

The service concluded quietly, the pews emptied with soft country talk and footsteps on the wooden floors. Outside, the air had warmed, the sun burned off the fog in streaks of golden hues.

Mike stepped out, letting the wind wash over him, the scent of earth mingling with the twang of sweat and summer blooms. He turned to see Q standing still on the chapel steps, eyes narrowed against the sunlight, a silhouette of stubborn loyalty.

Red lingered behind, her hands clasped loosely, eyes flicking between them both. She wanted to say something. Something to ease the tension. To remind them of boyhood laughter, the creek, the apple trees.

But she didn't.

Instead, she let them face each other as the weight of the land, the past, and Mrs. Lila Mae's memory pressed down like the midday sun.

Mike finally spoke, his voice low over the rustle of the crowd. "Q... I'm here, man. I'm back."

Q's jaws tightened even more. He didn't answer immediately. His eyes traced the lines of Mike's city suit, the shine of his polished shoes, the faint scent of cologne that felt wrong in this land he knew like the back of his hand. Finally, he let a short, sharp laugh escape.

"Thirty years later... hooray — you finally made it back."

The words were facetious, but the quiet weight behind them spoke of summers waited on, promises kept, and absences felt.

Cross caught the tension.

The pause.

The tone.

Her lips curled slightly, and her eyes flicked toward Sheriff Haskins. One subtle glance, and it said everything that was on her mind; *This is going to be easier than I thought.*

Q turned toward the stretch of land behind the chapel, as if signaling silently that the battle and the friendship were complicated now, layered with years and unspoken history.

Sheriff Haskins lingered at the edge of the crowd, lips pressed tight, his gaze drifting from Cross to the land.

Red followed the sheriff, understanding just enough to know that the stakes were no longer simply about land. They were now about loyalty, history, and what it meant to belong here.

Mike stepped onto the familiar dirt road, the wind brushing the sleeves of his jacket.

Some things hadn't changed.

Some things waited, patient and knowing, like the creek, the orchards, the red clay, and Q himself. All of it had a claim on him, whether he was ready to answer or not.

CHAPTER FIVE
The Dirt's Worth More

Dust rose in a thin cloud around Mike's car, marking it, claiming it, long before he saw Grandma Lila Mae's house waiting at the end of the dirt road.

The house smelled the same as it had when Mike was a boy. It almost looked the same, too. The scorching sun warmed the weathered wood of the porch, but inside the air felt cooler, older. The sweetness of pecans was still there, faint, like a memory that wouldn't quite come back to him. The smell of old wood and cold ash lingered in the chimney, more ghostly than fire.

Sunrays drifted through the lace curtains, and every creak of the floorboards sounded like a question he didn't know how to answer. It felt as if each piece of wood was screaming, like the house itself knew he had no right to be there.

He ran a hand along the banister, feeling the grooves his grandmother's palm had polished smooth over decades. A lump rose in his throat. He didn't belong here, not really, but it was becoming his now. That was the truth of it.

Hours passed before anyone spoke to him.

Mike stood inside the house longer than he meant to, letting the quiet marinate. The sun shifted across the floor.

Somewhere outside, a door slapped shut. A truck rumbled past on the road and faded. By the time he stepped onto the porch, the day had caught up with him.

Q was coming up the yard from the direction of the barn. He walked slow and calculated, boots cutting straight lines through the dust. His shoulders filled out his shirt now, wide and solid from years of lifting feed sacks and swinging tools. This was not the skinny boy with dirt on his cheeks and a stick in his hand. This was a man rooted here, one who moved like the land answered to him. When he reached the porch, he stopped close, close enough for Mike to feel it.

Q didn't offer a hand. He didn't smile. He just stood there, looking at Mike like someone assessing a fence line.

Before either of them could speak, a voice carried across the yard.

"Mike Berry. Long time."

Red was coming up the steps, a clipboard tucked under her arm, skirt and blazer pressed clean despite the heat. The beads and bows were gone from her braids, but the sharp spark in her hazel eyes was still there. She looked like she belonged in meetings and chambers now, not standing in the scorching sun of Country Acres.

"Red," Mike said, breath catching before he could stop it. "Hey. It's good to see you."

Q's head turned, just slightly.

"That's Councilwoman Parks," he said, flat and quick.

The words landed hard and heavy.

Red paused for half a second, then smiled, a small one. "It's alright, Q," she said.

Her eyes went back to Mike. "You can still call me Red."

Q didn't look at her when she said it. His eyes stayed on Mike, steady and unblinking, as if to say some names were only his to use, and some things had not changed just because time had passed.

Mike nodded, the city polish cracking as his smile turned really uncertain.

He understood then.

He was back on the land, but he was not home.

Red returned the look, soft but brief. Her eyes went to Q first, settling there like habit, before turning back to Mike.

"Good to see you, too" she said to Mike. Then, without looking back at Q, "Just wish it wasn't like this."

Before anyone could answer, the low hum of an engine rolled up the driveway. Gravel popped beneath the tires as a familiar sedan came to a stop near the house.

Reverend Brooks stepped out, black Bible tucked under one arm, his glasses perched low on his nose. He adjusted his jacket, then looked over the small gathering, his presence settling things without a word.

"Alright now," he said, voice steady, practiced. "Let's go on inside."

They followed him into the house.

The living room had been cleared of its clutter, chairs arranged in a stiff circle where laughter and conversation once lived.

Mike took a seat and sat straight, hands folded like he was afraid to touch anything.

Q perched on the edge of a chair, restless, knees spread, like a man ready to stand at the first wrong word.

Red folded her hands neatly in her lap, composed and watchful.

The screen door opened again, slower this time.

Two figures stepped inside.

The first was Dana Cross, the same unfamiliar woman from the funeral, dressed sharp and precise. Her presence cut through the room like a switchblade. Behind her came the sheriff, hat tipped low, boots heavy against the floorboards, moving through the house with a confidence that suggested he believed he belonged there.

Mike felt it then. This was no longer just a family matter. His brows lifted, slow and uncertain.

Across the room, Q rose to his feet, eyes fixed on the two strangers. He didn't speak. He didn't need to. The question settled thick in the air, heavy enough for everyone to feel it: *What were they doing here?*

Dana Cross didn't sit right away. She walked instead, slow, deliberate, fingers trailing along the back of Lila Mae's old kitchen chair like she was reading the grain of the wood.

"It's funny," she said, not looking at either of them, "how land remembers people longer than people remember each other."

Her eyes lifted to Mike. "You left."

Then to Q. "You had to stay."

She smiled, small and precise. "Magnolia is very good at finding which of those two choices costs more."

The shift didn't go unnoticed. Chairs creaked. The room had gone still, as if waiting to see what Q might do next.

Reverend Brooks cleared his throat, stepping forward.

"I know this is a lot right now," he said, voice calm but measured. "I'll explain everything. But first, let's all take a seat."

He lifted a thick folder, the edges worn from handling. He opened it, and the room seemed to lean in as his voice steadied.

"Mrs. Lila Mae Berry's last will and testament."

He paused once, as if to gather his soul, then continued.

"To my grandson, Michael Berry," the Reverend read, "I leave the house, the orchards, and every acre of land passed down to me. May you honor it as I have, and as our ancestors before us once did."

Mike's stomach knotted. He had expected it. Still, the weight of it settled heavy, like something living had climbed onto his shoulders and refused to move.

The Reverend paused, then continued, his voice gentler now.

"And to my dearest, Q. Though this land will not fully be yours by bloodline, know that my heart has always counted you as kin. You have worked this soil, guarded it, and loved it longer than anyone. For that reason, I direct that you and Mike hold this land together, as equal partners, fifty percent each."

A stir rippled through the small circle of chairs.

"The deed and final legal authority shall rest with Mike Berry," the Reverend continued to read, "but no choice concerning this land is to be made without the counsel and consent of Quan Richards."

The words landed unevenly.

A chair leg scraped against the floor.

Every head in the room turned, not together, but split.

Some eyes settled on Mike.

Others went to Q.

No one looked at the Reverend anymore.

"I ask that you stand as one," the Reverend read on, "and do not allow money, influence, or men from the outside to claim what was meant to be tended, not traded."

Silence.

Dana Cross exchanged a brief look with Sheriff Haskins. It was quick, sharp, and harsh. Their smiles didn't quite hold anymore.

Outside, the cicadas kept singing, careless of wills, land, or promises.

Ms. Cross leaned forward in Mike's direction, folding her hands as if in prayer. Her voice was smooth, and it cut clean through the room.

"I'm here because Magnolia, Inc. is prepared to purchase the land," she said. "Not for a fair price. For a substantial one. The kind of money that changes lives. Permanently, if you choose. Whether the town likes it or not."

The words were heavy.

Mike shifted in his chair. His chest tightened. Numbers lined themselves up in his head without asking permission.

Debt erased.

Futures secured.

Freedom bought.

Somewhere back in the city, a deadline was already waiting for his next move. He had made a life out of turning places into signatures on paper, and this land was already starting to ask for the same treatment.

The land was more than he could manage and Magnolia would pay him more than it was worth.

He opened his mouth.

"Maybe," he said carefully, "maybe selling isn't the worst idea. We could at least consid—"

"You just gon' outright sell it?" Q hissed.

His chair scraped hard against the floor as he sprung out of his seat. His voice came sharp, raw, like it had been waiting for permission to break loose.

"Like it's nothin'?" he continued. "She told you plain as day in that will, this land ain't for outsiders. And money made you forget that already? You forget the dirt? The oath? What we swore?"

He stepped closer now, eyes locked on Mike.

"You ain't no king," Q said. "You a damn fool."

Silence slammed down around them.

Mike swallowed, Q's words burning like a shot of bourbon whiskey. His chest locked up, feelings stinging as memory surged forward. Blood darkening the roots of the apple tree. Two boys, whispering promises they believed would last forever. He turned to Red, searching her face for guidance.

What he found wavered between two lives. One was the councilwoman, aware of what Magnolia's money could do for the town. The other was the girl who had watched two boys prick their thumbs and swear themselves kings of the dirt.

From her corner, Cross crossed her legs and smiled, just enough to show teeth. She said nothing, yet her presence pressed into the room.

The Sheriff stood behind her, hat tipped low. The two of them looked far too comfortable together.

Mike rose, the air thick between him and Q.

"I'm just saying," he said. "It's not that simple. Life isn't simple, Q. You can't hold on to dirt like it's worth more than what folks are offering."

Q's fists clenched.

"That dirt's worth more than this whole town," he said, sweeping his gaze around the room, locking eyes with each of them. "And y'all know it."

The Reverend snapped the folder shut. "That's enough for today, gentlemen," he said, firm and final. For a brief moment, his eyes settled on Mike, the weight in them unmistakable.

The gathering dissolved soon after.

Mike slipped out the back door, needing air. The orchards stretched before him, rows of pecan, pear, and apple trees, corn standing tall at the edges, all of it swaying under the evening wind.

He remembered chasing fireflies out there, carving promises into bark, burying a dog whose name still scarred a tree. His grandmother's voice surfaced, steady and clear.

Don't let money or men from the outside take it.

The weight hovered above his chest, heavier than any skyline he had ever stood beneath in Baltimore.

Q burst out the front of the house and stopped near the fence line, fists still clenched, eyes fixed on the trees like they might disappear if he looked away.

Red paused. She wanted to speak, to soften something sharp before it cut too deep. Instead, she met Q's eyes. Just a look. He gave her a single nod. He understood. So did she.

Dana Cross adjusted her cufflinks as she was escorted toward a waiting company limo, the sheriff falling in step beside her, both of them moving with the patience of people who knew they had time.

The last light of day filtered through the branches, casting long shadows down the aisles of trees and across the open fields.

Mike stood alone in the backyard, taking it all in.

Across the fields, Q sat on the tailgate of his pickup, eyes roaming the land he had spent his life tending.

A chill ran through his body.

The kind that came when something precious was already being measured, priced, and prepared to be taken.

51

CHAPTER SIX
Yesterday's Gone

The funeral day pressed heat into the skin and left the trees leaning like tired old men. By dusk, the air became cooler, cicadas rattling loud enough to drown out thoughts.

The orchards were quieter now, rows of fruit trees casting long shadows like ribs across the ground. A whippoorwill called from somewhere near Junction Lake, its song threading through the thick heat.

Magnolia's words still burned in Q's ears. *Life-changing money.* That was the devil's talk around these parts, dressed up in gold tie clips and promises that sounded too sweet. He kicked his boot against a low branch, the dull thud echoing his fury, yet the orchard's quiet made his memories louder.

He remembered running through these trees as a boy, barefoot and laughing, racing Mike and Red until his lungs burned. Back then, the trees were everything: battlegrounds, ladders, kingdoms of their own. He even remembered the apple tree down by the creek, bark carved with their initials, *Q+M+R*, a gang that swore it would never split.

Funny how that same bark looked cracked now, initials stretched thin, as if they too had grown apart over the years.

Inside, Mike had his notebook out, numbers scattered across the page like ants. His tie was off, sleeves rolled, but he still carried himself like the city slicker he had grown to become.

He pushed his pen down hard, pressing the tip till it nearly broke through the paper.

Magnolia Inc. Offer was scrawled across the top in bright red ink. Beneath it, long columns of figures, arrows, and possibilities.

The door creaked open. He glanced up, already expecting who it would be. Q stayed at the doorway, hands loose at his sides, but every inch of him screamed ownership. The room felt smaller and heavier now.

"Took you long enough," Mike said quietly, still scanning the columns of figures. "Come on in, Q."

Q got straight to it.

"You really think she meant for you to sit there chasin' numbers?" Q's voice came low, controlled, a warning more than a question. "You scribblin' dollar signs like that's what your grandma wanted?"

Mike's eyes landed on Q's. "I'm just thinking ahead. That land is worth more on paper than it will ever be worked. Magnolia is offering enough to give us both a real future."

Q barked a bitter laugh. "Ain't no future worth sellin' your soul, Mike." Then, he became more intense, "You forget fishin' down at the river? Pullin' brims and catfish? Haulin' watermelon in Old Man Willy's truck till our arms nearly broke?"

His stance shifted, casual replaced by rigid defiance. "Hell, for you it was only one summer. This dirt raised me. Magnolia don't care 'bout none of that. I guess you don't either."

Mike leaned back, the chair groaning under its weight. He dragged a hand down his face before speaking.

"I did not forget. Nostalgia does not pay bills. Magnolia is not going to just walk away because we stomp our feet. They have lawyers, investors, probably the whole council in their pocket."

The room felt smaller. The air thicker.

"We either sell and walk away clean, or we hang on and let them grind us into dust." His eyebrows raised. "You think I don't see what they're capable of?"

Silence pressed in.

Q didn't answer at first. He stepped forward instead. One slow step. Then another.

The floorboards creaked under his boots.

His fists clenched until the tendons stood out in his wrists.

"Walk away clean?" he said. "You already did. Thirty years ago. Left this place for big city lights and never looked back. And now you come struttin' in, actin' like you know what's best for land you ain't lifted a shovel on since you was knee-high to a grasshopper."

The words landed hard enough to knock the air from Mike's lungs.

Mike rose from the chair without meaning to. It scraped hard against the wood. They stood face to face now.

Mike's voice came sharp, city-cold.

"Do not put that over my head. I was a kid, Q. I left because summer ended. And while I was gone, you think you were the only one carrying weight? I built something too. Made something of myself, not just some country bumpkin."

Q went still. Not angry. Still.

The two stood silent, breaths heavy, the orchards dark and still outside the window. The space between them disappeared. And then, soft as a ghost, memory crept between them.

Mike glanced toward the stars over the trees. "You remember that night under the big oak tree by the river? Red brought marshmallows but forgot the sticks, so we roasted them on the nails from the shed."

Q cracked a half-smile, despite himself. "Yeah. You burned the first one so bad it looked like a lump of coal. Then swore you liked it that way."

Mike laughed, quick and bright, then it faded. He rubbed the back of his neck. "We were kids. I thought that summer would last forever."

Neither of them said what happened after.

Q nodded, eyes distant, tracing the dark lines of the orchards. "Feels like yesterday, but it ain't. Yesterday's gone, Mike. And now Magnolia's sniffin' around our tomorrow."

Before either could speak again, headlights cut across the room. A car door slammed. High heels clicked sharply on the ground. Red stepped through the front door.

She did not bother to sit. Her gaze found them immediately, sharp, assessing. She had their attention.

"Magnolia is up to no good. The council has been meeting with their people this evening. The town's already buzzing. Folks are saying you two won't be able to work together, and Magnolia reps are telling the council to give it time, so you'll crumble on your own. I'm not saying that you will. But you two better get it together before you lose it all."

Her eyes moved briefly between them, careful and measuring. She offered no judgment and no hint of taking a side. Her allegiance was subtle, but clear. She had roots here, and she knew what was at stake.

Then she left, just as quickly as she arrived.

Her words lingered, heavy as the humid evening air. Mike's energy shifted, tension coiling in his shoulders. Q turned toward the window, staring out into the orchard as if it could shield them both from what was coming.

Mike rubbed his temple, "I need some air."

Q's thoughts stopped racing for a moment, then he nodded. "Yeah. Gettin' a little stuffy in here anyway."

They stepped out together onto the back porch, the wooden boards creaking beneath their boots. Mike sank into the rail, the night air cooling his skin. Q leaned against the railing, arms crossed, the tension in his shoulders easing just slightly, but his eyes never left the orchard.

Q picked up Magnolia's glossy brochure, flipping it over in his hands. Pictures of smiling families, polished storefronts, and perfect tidy lawns stared back at him. He spat quietly to the side. "That's a lie dressed up as salvation," he said. He struck a match and held it to the edge, watching the paper curl into ash.

"They say they buyin' land," he said to Mike, "but what they really after is the people. They buyin' us out."

The ashes floated up into the night sky, fading among the stars.

CHAPTER SEVEN
Summer Don't Last Forever

Morning found Q by the fenceline behind the orchards, crouched low and fixing a busted gate hinge, when the faint smell of smoke reached his nose.

He paused.

It wasn't the clean, sweet smoke of hickory or oak. This was sharp, bitter, and wrong.

It burned his nostrils as it settled in, plastic and varnish mixing with something darker, something that tightened his stomach before his mind could catch up.

Q straightened up slowly.

A large shed sat just beyond the orchard line, its tin roof dulled by age, its wide doors scarred from decades of use. It had been Mrs. Lila Mae's nerve center. Everything that proved the land was theirs had once lived inside those walls.

Deeds.

Tax books.

Handwritten ledgers.

Old church minutes.

Contracts folded and refolded till the creases softened.

Q had spent countless afternoons inside those walls, hauling boxes, patching leaks, sweeping floors, listening to Lila Mae tell stories while the radio hummed low.

Then he saw it.

A thick gray plume rose from behind the shed, slipping into the morning sky like a signal meant only for him.

"No," Q muttered, already moving.

"Mike!" he hollered as he broke into a run. "Mike, get out here!"

The closer he got, the stronger the smell became. Burning papers. Melted plastic. Something sacred turning to ash.

Q kicked the shed door open.

Flames crawled along the base of the far wall, flicking at stacked boxes and old boards. One more minute and it would've reached the shelves. An antique picture frame lay half swallowed by fire, corner curling inward. Inside it, a photograph of Lila Mae stood trapped behind cracking glass. She was smiling, one hand on each boy's shoulder, back when time still felt generous and no one was measuring them.

Q didn't hesitate.

He ran for the porch, grabbed two fire extinguishers, and charged back in. White foam blasted across the flames, choking them down as smoke clawed at his throat and eyes. He coughed but kept spraying.

Mike burst in moments later. He yanked down a smoldering quilt from a hook and beat it into the dirt, striking it again and again until the last flame died out.

When it was finally over, the damage kept speaking. Ash drifted down slowly. The shed stood blackened but upright. The picture frame lay on the ground, glass shattered, the photograph inside scarred and blistered. The smell of burnt paper lingered, heavy and unforgiving.

Q stood there breathing hard, staring at what was left, already knowing something irreplaceable had been taken.

"What the hell happened?" Mike asked, chest heaving.

"I was about to ask you the same thing," Q said. He shook his head, eyes scanning the ground. "You smoke?"

"No," Mike said.

Q calculated for a moment. "This wasn't no accident. Fire don't start at the base of a wall like that."

He looked along the fence line, then toward the dirt road beyond the trees. "Somebody came out here before sunup. Won't do that again."

He nodded once to himself. "I'll be ready next time."

Mike knelt beside the burned remains and picked up the half-scorched photo. His thumb brushed what was left of Lila Mae's face. "Why this picture?" he asked.

Q didn't answer that. His jaws tightened harder, working like he was grinding down something bitter. His eyes stayed on the tree line.

Finally, he said it, low. "Magnolia."

Mike looked up fast. "You think they had something to do with this?"

"I think they been circlin'," Q said. "Ever since that will got read. Folks like that don't like hearin' no."

Mike frowned and stood, shaking his head. "That is a serious accusation. Nobody sets a shed on fire over a negotiation."

Q stepped closer, voice still calm but edged. "Over land worth more than this whole county? Over land they already been countin' as theirs?"

Mike turned away and paced. "We can't jump to conclusions without proof."

Q spat into the dirt. "You keep waitin' on proof, Cityboy, and you will be watchin' bulldozers roll through these orchards before Thanksgiving."

The words hung in the air just like the smoke did.

Q moved with sensitive steps through the soot. He crouched near the shed, running his fingers through the dirt, studying the scorch marks, the way the ash had settled. His eyes followed an invisible trail back toward the fence line.

"Fire didn't start here. It moved here." He pointed at a blackened hole in the ground. "You see this, don't you?"

Mike's shoulders sank. "Look, I don't want to argue with you, man. Not about this." He looked back at the shed, the blackened remains of their childhood hanging in the air. "But maybe this, whatever it is, is the universe telling us something."

Q gave a short, bitter smirk. "Yeah, it's tellin' us somebody wants us gone."

A distant rumble grew louder, and soon a lone fire truck was rolling down the dirt road, tires crunching over gravel. Q stepped back, arms crossed, as it pulled recklessly into the orchards.

The fireman, a stocky man with a familiar face to Q, climbed down from the truck.

"How ya doin', Q," he said, voice casual, almost too easy. "You must'a caught it quick. Prob'ly jussa' lectrical outlet. Happens all the time in old buildin's like 'dis."

He didn't step inside. Didn't crouch. Didn't smell the air.

Q crouched at the base of the shed, running a finger along the ash-stained ground, following the subtle trail that led away from the outlet. He didn't argue. He didn't have to. "Sure," he muttered, voice low. "That's real likely."

The fireman shrugged, nodded to Mike. "Betta' make sure nothin' else get caught. Could've been worse. I'll leave you boys to it." He tipped his hat and walked back to his truck as the engine rumbled to life before he drove off down the road.

Q stayed low, scanning the ground, searching every subtle clue the fire had left behind. Mike grabbed a broom, sweeping ash into a bucket, methodically and fast, like scrubbing away the memory along with the smoke.

They worked in a quiet rhythm, Q fixing the broken latch, Mike sweeping, while the sun sank behind the pear trees, casting a blood-red glow over the smoke. Q's eyes kept scanning the fence line and scorched wall, reading signs Mike didn't, or couldn't see.

Something wasn't right. The fire had taken more than wood and paper, it had whispered a threat they were only beginning to understand.

Mike was worn out, tired from nothing at all.

Q stayed locked in, scanning, watching, knowing.

***

Later, after Q had gone inside for the night, Mike stayed on the back porch, the crickets loud and the night thick with dew and memory. His hand drifted to the blackened photo frame lying on the ground from earlier. He picked it up carefully, still warm from the day's fire, and brushed the ash from the edges. The glass had cracked, but the image inside was mostly intact.

The portrait of Grandma Lila Mae smiling between young Mike and Q still stood. Somehow, it had survived.

As he turned the frame over, his fingers caught on something tucked behind the warped backing. A folded piece of paper, yellowed and brittle, had escaped the flames entirely. The glass and warped backing must have shielded it from the worst of the heat. He eased it out, careful not to tear it.

Looking across the field toward Q's house, he called out, "Q," but the only answer was the quiet night.

He held the letter up to the porch light. The first words were faint, but legible:

My boys. If you've come by this letter, it means I've gone home to glory, and the fate of Country Acres is now in your hands.

His heart skipped. He looked back toward the orchards, at the building where the smoke still lingered, and a quiet understanding settled over him.

This wasn't coincidence.

Grandma had planned for this.

Carefully, he folded the letter and tucked it into his jacket pocket, close to his chest. Whatever truth Grandma Lila Mae had hidden had survived the fire because it was meant for him to carry.

Out past the trees, unseen in the dark, a pair of headlights idled along the road for a moment too long, then vanished.

Even city eyes should have caught the warning, but Mike noticed nothing.

CHAPTER EIGHT
Grandma's Bible

The morning air sat heavy with dew and dust, broken only by cicadas stirring in the trees. Q was already outside before sunrise, standing near the old water hole.

The river ran low and slow this time of year, slipping between the reeds and catching what little light there was. Q skipped a stone across the surface and watched the ripples spread, then disappear. It comforted him.

Footsteps sounded behind him.

Mike walked up still wearing the clothes he had slept in, a folded paper clutched in his hand. "Found this in the ashes," he said quietly.

Q turned. "What is it?"

Mike stepped closer and unfolded the brittle paper with care. "It's from Grandma. She taped it behind a picture frame. It was tucked behind the backing. The glass must have shielded it."

They walked down to the dock and sat. Q took the letter, handling it like it might crumble in his hands.

As he read, Mike's eyes drifted past the water and locked onto the old apple tree by the bank. The one where they had carved their initials years ago, back when the days felt longer and nothing yet belonged to anybody else.

Q smoothed the letter open and began to read the graceful handwriting aloud.

"My boys. If you've come across this letter, it means I've gone home to glory, and the land is now in your hands. Don't ever forget what it's for. It don't belong to one man or to one company. It belongs to the people who worked it, prayed over it, and bled on it. Keep the land for the people. Not for the price. You two are special. I knew it since the day you met.

Inseparable. Do what's right. I know you will. With Love. Your Grandma."

His voice broke on the last word. He stopped, staring at the page. "Grandma," he said softly.

A tear rolled down his cheek. He didn't bother to wipe it away.

He sat there a long moment, then read the line again under his breath. "Keep the land for the people, not for the price."

He shook his head once.

"She used to say somethin' like that when I was little. Thought it was just one of her sayin's."

Mike leaned closer, eyes still on the paper. "Turn it over. There's more."

Q did, careful as before, and read on.

"The world will always offer you money to forget where you came from. But God's word says the land shall not be sold forever, for it is His, and we are but strangers and sojourners with Him."

"That's Leviticus," Mike said quietly.

"Twenty-five, twenty-three," Q answered without looking up.

Mike nodded, slow and thoughtful, his eyes shining. He had built his life on contracts and closings. This felt like something that couldn't be negotiated.

Q finally let some of the tension go. "Grandma used to quote that on our Sunday walks to church. Said the Lord gave us this ground to take care of, not trade off like a car title." He glanced at Mike. "That's what I wanted you to know. She was my grandma too. I loved her too. But she wouldn't have wanted this place sold off like it didn't mean nothin'. I hope you see that now."

They sat in the quiet a long while. The river moved slow beside them. Birds called from the trees. The letter rested between them like something living, fragile but full of weight.

Q leaned forward, hands working together without him noticing. "Did you find her Bible?"

Mike shook his head. "No. I haven't looked."

He wasn't sure he wanted to.

Q stood up at once, urgency settling into his face. Not panic. Purpose. "Then we need to. She didn't leave that letter alone for no reason."

Mike rose with him. "Alright," he said. "Let's go."

They didn't waste a second.

Boots thudded up the sun warmed porch. Hands gripped the rails as they pushed into Grandma Lila Mae's house. Dust rose in the sunlight slipping through the lace curtains, the quiet inside stirring like it had been waiting on them.

Mike went straight to the drawers, pulling them open, searching through stacks of aged papers and envelopes. He tore through drawers like a man chasing answers he could file and calculate.

Q moved slower, steadier. He checked behind cabinets, lifted couch cushions, and looked beneath mattresses. He moved like he was listening for something.

Neither said much. The urgency in their movements spoke for them. Two grown men chasing pieces of a woman who had shaped them both. They just went about it their own way.

Q pulled down the attic door and climbed the narrow steps, each one creaking under his weight. The attic smelled of old wood and long forgotten seasons. Dust clung to his skin as he took it in.

There was only one thing up there.

An old wooden box sat tucked against the far wall. Q's hands trembled just a touch as he lifted it. The hinges squealed when he opened it, like they were not meant to be rushed.

"Mike," he called, already heading back down. "I think I found somethin'."

They stood over the box together in the living room.

Inside were handwritten cookbooks, pages soft from use. Beneath them were folded papers, thicker, heavier. Q spread them out on the table.

Blueprints.

Not just of the house.

Of the land.

Country Acres.

Orchards mapped out by hand. Irrigation lines traced with care. Even outlines for buildings that did not exist yet, placed with intention, not greed.

Mike stared at them. "She planned all of this?"

Q nodded slowly. "Yeah. And she hid it where only we'd find it."

The box was clean, not dusty like the rest of the attic. It had been handled, not forgotten.

Mike ran his fingers over the pages, eyes widening. "Q... these blueprints are detailed. I don't even know half of this stuff."

He had spent years studying plans like these in conference rooms and glass towers. But these were different. These weren't meant to be flipped. They were meant to be finished.

He flipped through them, mind already racing. Zoning. Land use. Possibility. He didn't know whether he was looking at opportunity, or instruction. And for the first time, he wasn't sure which version of himself would win.

"I don't get it. Why would she have all this? What is valuable about blueprints and old Southern recipes?"

Q barely looked at the papers. His attention stayed on the room, on the corners, on what didn't belong.

"It ain't about value," he said. "It's about what she left us. What she wanted watched."

Mike stared at the spread of pages. For years, he had been the one who told people what their land was worth. Now it felt like the land was telling him what he was.

Q's eyes met Mike's. "We gotta find her Bible."

The words heavier than usual.

Q's gaze drifted toward the back of the house, toward the building beyond the window. The blackened wood still smoked faint, even in daylight.

"The fire," he said, realization tightening his voice.

They moved.

Boots crunched over gravel and ash as they reached the shed. The smell of burned paper and varnish hit hard, clinging to the back of the throat. Q pulled the latch and swung the door open.

What remained was ruin. Charred boards. Blackened beams. Ash settled into the dirt like snow.

Q knelt, shifting scorched wood aside, careful, patient. Then his hand stopped.

"There," he said, barely above a whisper. "Grandma's Bible."

It sat where it had fallen, leather cover darkened but intact, the pages spared where the flames had not fully reached.

Q lifted it slowly, cradling it in both hands.

For a moment, he didn't speak. He just stood there, breathing, holding it close like something living.

Mike watched. Something twisted in his chest. Not anger. Not exactly. Something sharper. Older.

"She wasn't even your grandma," he said.

The words landed wrong the moment they left his mouth.

Q drew in a slow breath, then let it out through his nose. He did not turn right away. When he did, his eyes locked on Mike, cold and dark, the kind of look that warned you not to test what lived behind it.

"I'm gon' let that one slide," he said. "But don't mistake that for weakness. She raised me same as blood. And I will lay a man out over my grandma."

Mike swallowed, shame rushing through his veins. He stepped back, rubbing the back of his head, eyes dropping. "That's not what I meant," he said quietly. "I just... I wasn't here. I should have been."

Q didn't press it. He turned toward the house. "Let's get this inside."

They carried the Bible back, setting it on the kitchen table like something sacred.

Mike drifted to the box they'd opened earlier, flipping through the cookbooks and papers with a quiet fascination, giving Q space. Notes scribbled in the margins with details of pecan preservation, cornbread sauces, and precise measurements hinted at more than recipes. It wasn't just cooking. It was planning.

"These could sell," Mike said, eyes lit. "High-end. Restaurant grade. My neighbor in Baltimore just graduated from a Michelin-star program. Sous chef. Could take these recipes and—"

Q raised an eyebrow, letting the look do the talking. "The only Michelin we know 'round these parts is treaded on all-weather tires."

Mike laughed, a little sheepish, but still excited. He turned another page in the cookbook, realizing there was more there than just recipes.

For a moment, they allowed themselves a small, silent revel in what they had uncovered. The Bible. The blueprints. The recipes. It was like Grandma Lila Mae had left them a treasure map, each piece carefully placed for the right hands to find.

And somewhere in the back of their minds, the possibilities began to form. Unspoken. Untouched. For now, it was discovery. For now, it was theirs.

Q opened the Bible carefully, its spine soft from decades of Sundays and Grandma's calloused hands. He held it like it might crumble if handled wrong. Near the front, around Leviticus, his thumb caught on something thicker than the surrounding pages. A small packet, folded precisely, pressed between the thin, yellowed sheets.

He eased it out slowly.

The Bible had held it all this time, tucked in as if it were just another page, but deliberate, intentional. Like Mrs. Lila Mae had known they'd need it.

Mike leaned in closer, eyes wide. "What is that?"

Q didn't answer right away. He lifted the packet just enough to feel the weight of it in his hands.

The paper was crisp but aged, stacked in careful order. Deeds. Survey maps. Copies of certified letters.

Court filings stamped and dated. Environmental assessments with sections highlighted in red ink. The dates stretched back nearly fifty years.

Magnolia Inc.'s letterhead appeared again and again.

An offer to purchase ten acres along the creek in 1978, declined.

A 1986 request to reclassify the orchard land as "underutilized agricultural property."

A 1994 zoning petition proposing a "mixed-use development corridor" cutting straight through the eastern pecan line.

Tax reassessments that spiked suddenly in years following each refusal.

A 2003 notice questioning the structural integrity of outbuildings.

A 2011 environmental inspection request citing "possible watershed mismanagement."

And beneath it all, a draft filing referencing eminent domain, contingent on county approval for expansion.

Each document was paper-clipped to handwritten notes in Lila Mae's careful script.

Denied.

Appealed.

Filed response.

Do not sign.

This wasn't interest.

This was patience.

Mrs. Lila Mae had seen them coming decades ago. Not loud. Not reckless. Methodical. Waiting for age, for weakness, for the right heir to falter.

And now she had placed the history in their hands, hidden in plain sight, so the fight would not start blind.

Mike ran a hand down his face. This wasn't a negotiation anymore. It was a campaign. And he had almost handed them the final signature.

His breath caught up. "Grandma... she was fighting them. The whole time. She left all this for us to find?"

He sat back slowly. This wasn't a simple inheritance anymore. This was a war he had just walked into on the wrong side of.

Q shook his head. Up and down, twice.

He didn't hear her voice exactly. Not words. Just the memory of her standing in the orchard at dusk, hands on her hips, chin lifted, watching the tree line like it owed her an explanation. The way she would squint at the road when strange cars passed. The way she always folded letters before sliding them into her apron pocket.

He could see her now in that kitchen chair, Bible open, finger pressed to the page like she was daring the world to try her.

His eyes finally lifted, scanning the room and the land beyond.

"She planned for this," he said. "Knew we'd have to see it ourselves. Know it was real before we believed it."

Mike swallowed hard, awe and fear twisting in his chest. "She... she knew we'd need it. That we'd have to fight."

Q nodded, reverent but steady. "She did. And if we don't, it'll all be for nothin'. But if we do... we do it the right way."

He ripped open the last document, a report marked **CONFIDENTIAL**.

Chemical runoff.

Soil contamination.

Forced sales.

Land lost not to thieves, but to paperwork.

"They didn't just buy up the land," he said quietly. "They starved folks out."

Mike sank into the chair across from him.

One document showed Magnolia suing a farmer for code violations. Another showed the same land condemned months later. A third tied the site to buried waste, dumped just far enough upstream to poison crops without ever landing on Magnolia's property.

"They used the law like a rope," Q went on. "Wrapped it slow. Pulled it nice and tight, till folks couldn't breathe. That's why Sheriff Haskins following behind that rep. She got him in her pocket."

Mike ran a hand down his face.

"And Grandma knew," he whispered.

Q tapped the page they were on. "That's why she marked this chapter. Leviticus 25. Jubilee. The return of the land. Freedom from debt. She's tellin' us where to look. She's pointing us somewhere."

Silence hovered between them, thick and heavy, broken only by the cicadas outside starting their afternoon chants.

Mike swallowed hard, pride broken.

He sank into the chair.

"I didn't see this," he said quietly. "I didn't know."

He stared at the papers again.

"I saw numbers. An exit. A clean win."

He looked up at Q.

"I didn't see the bodies underneath it."

He met Q's eyes, city polish gone, just a man left. "I shouldn't have talked about selling it like that."

Q studied him for a moment, then exhaled.

"Took you long enough, Cityboy," he said.

Mike let out a weak breath that might've been a laugh. "Guess the country had to beat it into me."

Q folded the documents back into the Bible and closed it gently. "She picked you too, ya' know. Ain't no accident you came back when you did. She knew you'd come to honor her life."

Mike nodded, eyes burning from holding back thirty years' worth of tears.

Q stood first. Mike followed. They didn't say much. They didn't need to. They stood there a moment longer than necessary, neither sure who moved first.

The hug came solid and brief, the kind men give when words would only get in the way. Shoulders firm. Grounded. Solid.

Q walked to the kitchen, opened the fridge and pulled out two cold beers. They stepped out onto the porch and sat side by side, the orchards stretching out in front of them, rows of trees standing quiet and patient.

Q popped the caps. Handed one over.

"To land that don't break. Roots that won't shake," he said.

Mike clinked bottles. "To Country Acres."

They drank in silence as the sun drifted lower, Leviticus 25 resting on the table between them. No longer just a Bible, but a confirmation.

And somewhere deep in the soil beneath their feet, something long buried had finally started to rise.

The weight of all this history, responsibility, and promise settled over them at the same time as the warm southern sun, and for a second, there was a silence that felt sacred between the two men.

Then the crunch of tires over gravel shattered it. Headlights swept across the yard, slicing through the late afternoon shadows.

Mike and Q exchanged a quick glance, instincts sharpening, working in tandem. The SUV door opened, and out stepped Dana Cross, clipboard in hand, city documents tucked neatly under her arm. Two men in hard hats followed, their eyes scanning the shed and orchards with precise, almost clinical focus.

"Gentlemen," Ms. Cross said, polite but sharp, every word measured, "the fire burned through an old storage structure on the property. Preliminary inspection indicates elevated levels of nitrates and trace heavy metals in runoff soil samples near the shed site. That puts the entire orchard at risk of contamination."

She tapped her folder once.

"State agriculture law requires the land to be cleared, tested, and remediated before any produce can be sold or distributed. Seven days to submit certified testing and remediation plans, or the county will suspend your agricultural license."

She clicked the pen against her clipboard, the sound echoing like a gunshot. "Here's your copy, signed by City Council President, Candace Parks."

Her eyes slid to Mike, icy and calculated, "I believe you call her Red."

She finished, "once the state flags produce as unsafe," she added, "it doesn't come back from that easily."

Q's eyes shuffled through the screen door, locking on all the scattered documents and Bible lying on the table. A sense of threat rolled over him like a heavy tide. He glanced at Mike, and for the first time since coming back, Mike felt the full weight of what it meant to guard the land.

"Get off my property, now," Mike said, voice steady even as adrenaline surged.

"You've got seven days. So do we."

Q's lips curved into a faint, approving smile. "Bout time you came aroun', Cityboy," he muttered, a flash of brotherly pride in his eyes. Side by side, they stared at the shed, the orchard, and the land that had raised them.

Watching the Magnolia SUV disappear down the road, they both knew it was not over. Whoever Magnolia sent next, whatever threats came with them, Mike and Q were now ready.

They stood there until the dust settled. Neither spoke. The orchard looked the same. But it wasn't.

Q finally felt like he wasn't standing alone. Mike felt the weight of his grandmother's legacy settling into his hands, heavy but right. The land didn't feel inherited anymore. It felt contested. And neither Magnolia nor any state law was taking this land without a fight.

Q's phone chimed, sharp against the quiet yard. He checked the screen once. That was all it took. He locked the phone and slid it into his pocket like it might burn through his palm. He looked back toward the road, toward the bend where the SUV had vanished. Then at Mike.

"Get dressed," he said.

Mike caught the shift immediately. No jokes. No explanation. Just purpose.

"Where are we going?"

Q was already in motion. "Pool hall. Leavin' at eight-thirty."

CHAPTER NINE
Seven Days

The pool hall used to be an arcade back when they were kids and summer still meant something. Mike remembered that much the moment he stepped inside.

The smell had changed. Less grease and candy now. More beer and chalk. The warped floor near the back wall was still there. The low hum of machines had been replaced by the click of balls and the dull thud of cues breaking the silence.

The country introduced itself quietly around here. It did not rush you. It let you sit down and decide who you were going to be.

Red was already inside, leaning against the far table beneath the humming fluorescent lights. No blazer tonight. Just jeans, boots, and a plain white top tucked clean at the waist.

Still sharp. Still Red. But grown now in a way that made Mike hesitate, like he was staring at a memory that had learned how to stand on its own.

Q nodded once when he saw her. No smile. No hug. Just respect.

"Always prompt and on time," she said, racking the balls with a natural ease. "Thanks for coming, Q."

Mike noticed the way she moved. Measured. Confident. Not the girl who used to beat them both at Mortal Kombat and laugh about it. His chest stirred with something old and unhelpful before he could stop it.

She broke hard. Balls scattered across the table. The crack echoed through the room like a warning shot.

"You know I didn't want to sign those papers," Red said, lining up her next shot. "But if I hadn't, Magnolia would have had them signed by somebody else in the morning. This way, I bought you seven days instead of one."

Mike crossed his arms. "Seven days to lose everything."

Red didn't even look at him. She sank the ball clean. "Seven days to prove they don't get to steal what ain't theirs."

Q leaned against the table, eyes steady on Mike. "She did what she had to do."

Mike scoffed. "Funny how had to always looks the same when money involved."

Mike's cue tip pressed too hard into the felt, leaving a faint blue scar.

That did it.

Q straightened, voice low but firm. "Watch yourself, Mike."

Mike turned. "I'm just saying, how are we supposed to trust information from somebody who just put the clock on our land?"

Red set her stick down slow. Deliberate. She met Mike's eyes for the first time.

"Because I grew up on that land too," she said. "Because I buried folks there. Because Grandma Lila Mae fed me when my mama couldn't."

She paused, gathered herself, lowered her voice.

"How do you think she got access to confidential files."

Mike froze.

"She didn't just wake up knowing Magnolia's dirt," Red went on. "She went out and dug it up. Built herself a seat at tables they tried to keep her from. And when I didn't yet know how this game was played, she taught me how to play it back."

Silence spread between them.

"Magnolia has been sniffing around here for years," Red said. "They never thought anyone out here knew how to read what they leave behind."

Q didn't take his eyes off Mike. "Loyalty ain't about who signs papers," he said. "It's about who stays when it get ugly."

Mike exhaled. His shoulders dropped an inch. "Alright," he said quieter. "Alright. I hear you."

Red softened then, just a touch. "Here is the truth. Magnolia is claiming environmental hazard. Fire residue. Accelerants. If the land ain't cleared and certified in seven days, they file emergency seizure. You lose the inheritance outright."

Mike's stomach sank.

Q nodded, already thinking. "Then we clean it up. Get it back to code."

Red raised a brow. "You two can't do it alone."

"We won't," Q said, his confidence settled and certain. "Country Acres still knows us. We Lila Mae's boys. I can get folks moving in the morning."

Mike watched him.

Really watched him.

They played another game. Then another.

Mike laughed when Red beat him with a bank shot that felt personal. "Dang girl, you always been cold like that."

She smirked. "Some things don't change."

Others had.

He felt it then. The distance. She spoke to Q like kin. Like shared blood that was never written down. And Mike found himself standing in that old familiar place again.

The guest. The grandson. The outsider.

Q's phone buzzed once. He ignored it. Buzzed again. He stopped.

Mike noticed before Q said anything. The way Q's shoulders locked. The way his grip tightened around the phone like it might fight back. The focus sharpening in his eyes.

"What is it?" Mike asked.

Q looked down. The screen's glow washed his face pale, drained something out of him.

"Trail cam," Q said, already zooming in.

The video loaded, then played.

Two men moved along the orchard line, their bodies washed gray in infrared light. Their jackets were zipped high against their chins. Reflective stitching caught the glow of the camera. On the left chest of each jacket, the Magnolia Inc. logo was visible. A letter "M" and a magnolia bloom stitched in white thread. Clear. Distinct. Impossible to mistake.

One of the men turned slightly, and the logo flashed brighter as he shifted.

Each of them carried something heavy in one hand. Metal swung at their sides as they walked.

Gas cans.

Mike leaned closer, his stomach turning. "That's on our property?"

Q ain't answer that. His eyes filled with wrath.

He grabbed Mike's arm, hard enough to sting.

"We gotta go."

"Q—"

"Now, Mike!"

Q was already moving. No explanation. No warning. He pushed through the door and headed straight for the truck.

Mike followed, pulse climbing, questions piling up behind his teeth.

Red stayed where she was, cue stick resting against her leg. She had seen that look on Q's face before. Rare. Dangerous. The kind that meant something bad was already in motion.

They were gone before she could say a word. Some things, she knew, were still theirs to carry alone.

Q's truck roared to life and tore out of the lot, tires screaming on pavement before biting into gravel.

As the road narrowed, Q didn't slow down. He veered off before the turn that led deeper into town, cutting left, then right, then slipping onto a dirt path so thin it barely registered as a road at all. Branches clawed at the sides of the truck. Brush scraped metal. The land closed in around them.

Mike braced himself, gripping the door handle. "Q, are they really on the property?"

Q didn't slow down, eyes fixed on the path ahead. "Trail cam don't lie, Cityboy. Been locked in all day. That's them."

Mike swallowed hard, heart banging like a drum. "You've been watching this all day?"

"Yep," Q said flatly. "Just like I promised I would."

Before the orchard line came into view, Q cut the engine. The truck rolled forward in silence, tires crunching soft dirt, then settled to a stop. The headlights went dark.

Q leaned across the seat, his voice barely a breath. "From here on out, don't say a word."

Mike nodded.

They stepped out into the night, boots sinking slightly into damp ground. Crickets filled the air.

Something moved deeper in the trees. Q reached back into the cab and pulled out his shotgun, calm and sturdy.

Then the smell hit him.

Not wood smoke. Not leaves.

Kerosene.

Thick. Bitter. Wrong.

Mike sniffed once, then whispered, "That's what we smelled yesterday."

Q nodded. "Yeah."

They moved forward low and slow, letting the trees swallow them. The orchard opened ahead, rows of pecan trees standing quiet and watchful.

Two men stood near the center row.

One chuckled under his breath. The other tilted a gas can, dark liquid splashing against the roots of a tree Q had climbed a thousand times as a boy.

The man stepped back.

The other struck a match.

The sound was small. The flare was not.

Q lifted the shotgun as he moved, steady and deliberate, the motion as natural as his walk.

Mike's breath caught in his throat.

"DON'T MOVE," Q thundered, stepping forward, gun locked on them. "NOT ONE STEP."

Mike stood beside him, heart hammering as the truth settled heavy in his chest.

They hadn't imagined it.

They hadn't overreacted.

This wasn't business anymore.

It was war.

Down the road, porch lights flicked on. Dogs started barking. Country Acres stirred, roused by the sound of a line being crossed.

Q didn't lower the gun. Something inside him had shifted, and he knew there was no walking back across it.

Mike didn't step back.

Standing shoulder to shoulder in the dirt that raised them, the land seemed to recognize something too. They weren't running. Not tonight.

BOOM!

The blast split the orchard in half.

Birds erupted from the trees in a violent rush.

The man folded backward, the gas can slipping from his hand. He hit the dirt and did not move. Not a twitch. Not a breath. The match burned out before it could finish what it started.

Silence swallowed the rows of trees.

Smoke curled from the shotgun barrel.

Mike couldn't turn away. He stared at the body in the dirt. The stillness was wrong. Permanent.

This wasn't a warning shot.

This wasn't a scare tactic.

Q had meant it.

Something in Mike's chest gave way. The porch arguments, the paperwork, the numbers in his notebook. None of that existed here.

This was blood in the dirt.

This was a line drawn that could not be erased.

He wasn't visiting anymore.

He was standing in it.

Q lowered the barrel an inch, eyes steady, breathing even. He didn't look at the body. He had already decided.

He shifted the barrel, smooth and unhurried, bringing it level with the second man's chest.

The man didn't run. He couldn't. The shotgun froze him where he stood, like the dirt itself had told him he wasn't going anywhere.

Without breaking eye contact, Q spoke. Low and steady.

"Mike. Call 9-1-1. Tell 'em somebody's been shot out here in Mrs. Lila Mae's pecan orchard. Then hang up. Don't give 'em nothing else."

Mike's hands shook as he pulled out his phone. "I'm on it," he said, already dialing.

Q kept the barrel trained on the man.

"Mr. Magnolia," he said, voice calm as the ground beneath his boots. "Call Cross. Tell her every 'thang went according to plan."

He leaned in closer, the muzzle never wavered.

"Then hang it up."

The man didn't hesitate.

He dialed.

CHAPTER TEN
How Business Gets Handled

The town woke up before the sun. Not all at once. Not because of lights, alarms, and sirens. It woke the way only the country knew how. Through vibration. Through whispers faster than reason. Through phones buzzing on nightstands, kitchen counters, and dashboards already pointed toward work.

Red had just jumped out of bed. Barefoot in the kitchen, coffee machine brewing, she watched the night sky loosen its grip as the sun waited just out of sight.

Her phone buzzed. Then again. Then again. Then it wouldn't stop.

She ignored the first two calls. She already knew something had happened. In towns like this, bad news didn't knock. It leaned against the door, waiting to be noticed.

The third call came from the City Clerk.

Red answered. No hello. No comfort greeting. All business.

"Yes?"

A careful pause. Breathing. Papers shuffling.

"There was... an incident last night," the clerk said.

Red closed her eyes.

"Is anyone hurt?"

A longer pause.

"One man's dead," the clerk said. "Another's in custody."

Red opened her eyes, staring at the road, dark with dew and laid bare.

"Which property?" she asked.

The clerk didn't answer immediately. That was answer enough. She stood there, her hand tightened around the counter until her knuckles went pale.

She didn't need names. Didn't want confirmation. In her bones, she already knew it was Q and Mike out there in the dark, tangled in whatever truth had finally come to light. She just didn't know which one had paid the higher price.

"It's them orchards," the clerk said. "The ones Magnolia's been sniffin' around since that old woman died."

The dagger.

***

Across town, Sheriff Haskins sat alone in his office, hat resting on the corner of his desk like it didn't want to be there either.

The smell of his coffee had gone cold. The radio playing soft jazz music, barely audible to the ears.

He'd already made his final report. Already logged the body. Already booked the surviving man on trespassing and attempted arson charges.

His phone rang.

He let it ring three times before answering.

"Sheriff Haskins," he said, already rushing to end the conversation ahead.

Dana Cross didn't waste time.

"Sheriff Haskins," Cross said, her voice clipped. "I got your message. Are you saying one of my contractors is in custody?"

Haskins leaned back in his chair, eyes drifting to the window, tracing the tree line beyond the station. "That's correct. Caught on private property in the

98

middle of the night with kerosene accelerants. One of Magnolia, Inc.'s men."

A sharp edge crept into her tone. "That's impossible. My men confirmed nothing happened. Surely, you're mistaken."

Haskins didn't flinch. "I'm not mistaken. One of your men won't be needing bail. He's... deceased."

There was a pause. Not shock. Not grief. Cross' mind raced, calculating. "Deceased? That's a lie, Sheriff. My team confirmed—"

"No reason to lie," Haskins cut in, voice low and steady. "The body's at the coroner's office. He was shot on private property after attempting arson. No mistake. No misreporting. Just facts."

"That complicates timelines," she said. "But these things happen when emotions run high. I'll have legal send over paperwork. I expect my man released by noon."

Haskins straightened.

"No ma'am," he said.

The words sat heavy between them. A boundary. Something newly introduced between the two.

Cross exhaled slowly. "Sheriff, let's not complicate this."

"It already is," Haskins said.

Another pause.

"I have records, Sheriff" she said. "Payments. Campaign donations routed through subsidiaries. Off-record property contributions. Things ethics boards tend to misunderstand."

Haskins closed his eyes for a moment.

When he opened them, his voice was different. Older. Rooted.

"You threatenin' me, Ms. Cross?"

"I'm reminding you," she said, "where your loyalty has historically landed."

Haskins stood.

The chair scraped loud against the floor.

"My loyalty," he said, "has always been right here. To the town folk who elected me as Sheriff to protect and serve. Honorably."

She waited.

Haskins straightened up, the weight of authority filling his voice. "Sheriff's orders: I'm not arrestin' a man for standin' on his own dirt. And I damn sure won't let Magnolia burn this county to salt so y'all can put up another sign."

The line went dead.

Haskins set the phone down, slow, like it might explode soon.

***

Red burst through the doors at City Hall. The council members moved as if nothing had changed, going through the motions of a normal day. But their faces were tight and the air felt heavy with tension.

No one said Magnolia's name out loud. But everyone thought it.

Emails came in from environmental oversight. The zoning department requested clarification.

A junior councilman leaned forward. "There was an incident on the Berry orchards last night. I believe the current condition of that land needs to be reviewed by this council before any further decisions are made."

Red said nothing. She was the President. She had to be neutral. She had to remain poised.

So, she listened.

She watched the way the power shifted around the room.

She watched everything and everybody, not knowing who to trust. She stayed collected and completed the meeting, but not without a lot of hesitation.

Once she adjourned the meeting around noon, she drove past the orchards.

She didn't stop. Didn't pull in. Didn't interfere.

She didn't want to.

Red kept driving, heart heavy.

Q stepped outside and caught sight of Red's car rolling past in the distance. She didn't slow down. Didn't stop. That wasn't like Red.

"Mike," Q called out. "Call Red. Ask her why she just drove by and ain't speak."

Mike pulled out his phone.

Q's eyes stayed fixed on the road. "Tell her every 'thang. But keep it short. She can't get caught up in this. Not yet."

"Got it," Mike said as he dialed.

Red answered on the first ring, her voice tight and sharp. "Mike? What happened last night?" Her voice cracked, panic leaking through. "Did Haskins let you call? Who's dead? Is Q alive? What happened out there?"

"It's a long story, Red," Mike said carefully.

She cut him off. "Well, tell me."

Mike did his best. He gave her the pieces that mattered and left the rest where it belonged. No names that didn't need saying. No details that would drag Q or the land deeper than it already was.

On the other end, Red's grip tightened on the steering wheel. It was all too familiar.

The fires. The pressure. Magnolia circling land they did not own and calling it business. She had seen this play before, years ago, from the edges, from the shadows, standing beside people who never got credit for holding the line.

"They're doing it again," she said quietly, more to herself than to Mike. Anger gave way to something sharper. Recognition. "Same tactics. Same timing."

She swallowed. "And if Haskins let this escalate..."

The thought trailed off unfinished.

"I'll call you back," she said.

The line went dead.

Almost fumbling, Red dialed the sheriff. No answer.

She tried again. Still nothing.

She cursed under her breath as realization set in. Haskins was choosing his own path now. Whether that meant silence, distance, or something worse, she didn't know yet. Only that something had shifted.

Back at the house, Q didn't look at Mike when he asked, "What'd she say?"

"She mentioned Haskins," Mike said. "Said she'd call me back."

Q exhaled slow. "She sees it now. Let her be."

Mike swallowed. "She sounded angry."

"Good," Q said, voice low, almost a growl.

***

The story had broke the way it always did in the country, through rumor and whisper, spreading like wildfire.

By the time the first rooster crowed in Country Acres, radios were already running the same poisoned lines.

A building burned. Questions raised. Two heirs at odds. Money involved. Land at stake.

Cross made sure of that.

The article ran in three regional outlets before daylight. Same language. Same tone. Just dressed up differently depending on who was reading it.

Suspicious fires on disputed property. Insurance fraud. Evidence allegedly destroyed. Dead Body Discovered.

It painted Q as reckless. Territorial. Dangerous. It painted Mike as greedy. Calculating. A city man ready to cash out once the smoke cleared. Together, the narrative said they were what Magnolia needed them to be.

Unstable.

By seven a.m., folks were reading it on their phones while coffee brewed and grits popped.

By eight, they were hearing it from neighbors.

By nine, it was on the local news station, polished smoothly, as if it were true.

Q stood at the edge of the orchard and listened.

Not to the radio. To the land.

The ground on the orchards was dark and wet, but the smell still lingered, sharp and wrong. Kerosene always told on itself.

Mike walked up beside him, phone in hand. "They're saying we're the problem."

Q nodded once. "That part there easy to believe."

"They say I planned to sell."

Q finally looked at him. "Well, are you?"

"No."

Q turned back toward the orchards. "Then we done talkin' bout it."

A vehicle crunched over gravel out front.

Both men froze.

The sound didn't belong to the land. Tires too careful. Engine idling where it shouldn't. Q shifted, eyes cutting toward the house.

The fire inspector arrived.

"Morning, Mr. Richards. Mr. Berry. Just here to follow up on the investigation."

They stepped into the house, eyes fixed on the fire inspector through the screen door, neither of them saying a word.

The man didn't rush. He walked slowly, knelt often, took samples, photographed patterns. He said little and wrote plenty.

By noon, he had all the answers that he needed.

The accelerant was powerful. A special mix of kerosene, overly concentrated. Pooled in places fire did not start on its own. The burn pattern showed intention, not accident.

By mid-afternoon, Mr. Halcomb at the farm supply store had already made two phone calls.

He remembered the purchase. Twenty gallons of industrial kerosene. Not the kind folks used for heaters. The contractor had asked too many questions about burn rates. Paid in cash. Didn't want it rung up under the company account.

Halcomb still had the carbon copy of the receipt in his drawer. Magnolia contractor. Signed three days before the shed burned.

By evening, neighbors' trail cam footage began circulating the way things do in small towns. Carefully. Person to person. Time stamped. Two figures moving through the trees well before the fire would have started. Wasn't Q. Wasn't Mike.

That was when the story started to crack.

Not online. Not yet.

In kitchens.

At the local feed stores.

On tailgates and front porches.

Farmers recognized it immediately.

"That's that city mess again," they whispered.

Old heads leaned back in their chairs and shook their heads. They had seen this before. Pressure dressed up as concern. Fire used as fear. Stories planted early so the truth never had room to breathe.

An environmental memo meant for the zoning subcommittee was forwarded to three orchard owners before lunch.

A timestamped still from a trail cam showed up in the group chat the farmers used during harvest season.

No official announcement. No press conference. Just paper and proof, moving the way it always had in Country Acres.

A man who lost his land ten years ago finally spoke up. Then another. Then another.

Magnolia didn't invent the tactic, they just perfected it.

By sunset, the article was still up, but the tone around town had shifted. Folks stopped repeating the story and started questioning it. Quietly at first.

Q noticed it when Mr. Dillard slowed his pickup instead of speeding past.

When old Mrs. Kenner waved instead of looking away.

When nobody asked him what happened, but everybody nodded like they already knew.

The land hadn't turned on him. That mattered.

Dana Cross had played her first hand loud and early. She wanted panic. She wanted division. Wanted the folks to believe the land was already lost.

Instead, she reminded them why they did not trust outsiders who talked pretty and burned things in the dark.

The fire didn't destroy the truth.

It lit it up.

And Country Acres was watching now.

***

Miles away, Dana Cross sat behind the sleek black conference table, the city skyline glaring back at her through floor-to-ceiling windows. She adjusted her blazer and smoothed her hair. Across from her, five men in crisp, black, suits tapped their fingers on polished surfaces, eyes sharp, impatience leaking from every crease.

"Dana," the tallest one said, voice flat and cold, "we need results. You're telling us that Country Acres isn't cooperating, and you know that entire town is pivotal. If you can't close this city, we can't move on to Phase Two. You understand what that means for you."

She nodded, a practiced smile on her face. "I understand completely."

"Do you? Because right now, you're letting a small town of country bumpkins dictate terms to a corporation that could make us all millionaires."

Cross leaned back, folding her hands. "Gentlemen, the pieces are in place. Articles have gone out this morning, painting the heirs as the reckless fools that they are. The inspection process is being handled appropriately. I'm confident his report will favor our angle."

The men exchanged looks. One tapped his pen sharply. "And what if he doesn't?"

Her smile didn't falter, though a flicker of unease passed through her eyes. "He will. At this stage, there's nothing to worry about. All the optics are ours. The community won't even see the moves coming."

A pause. The tallest executive leaned forward. "That land sits above a stable aquifer and three fiber corridors. We can cool servers there for half the cost of Atlanta. Crops don't scale. Infrastructure does. You either deliver, or you're out. Understand?"

"Yes, I understand," Cross said, voice calm, smooth. Too smooth.

One of the men leaned back, fingers steepled. "You're fiesty and tenacious, Dana. Reminds me of your mother when she was running this division. But... you're trailing just a touch behind her pace."

Dana's jaw tightened imperceptibly, lips pressed together. She nodded once, keeping her smile steady. "I'll catch up."

She closed her tablet with a practiced click, signaling the end of the meeting. She rose, straightened her skirt, and offered a nod to the executives. "Consider it handled."

Once alone in the elevator, she leaned against the mirrored wall, staring at her reflection.

As the elevator doors closed, she immediately dialed the fire inspector. The line clicked, and his voice came through, calm but firm.

"Hello"

"What did you find?"

"Ms. Cross," he said, "I need to ask a few questions before I can sign off on anything."

There was no hesitation in his tone, only steady authority.

"The accelerant pattern doesn't match, nor support accidental spread. The timestamps don't match your submission. And I've reviewed the trail cam footage."

She tried to keep her voice smooth. "I can make it worth your while if it starts matching up" she said, a subtle edge of threat hidden beneath her words.

The inspector ignored that.

"I didn't ask for anything you've given me, Ms. Cross. My job is to do right by the law and by the people I serve. That's enough for me."

Her stomach tightened. Could it be possible... he was siding with them? With Q and Mike?

Had Country Acres started winning? No. She refused the thought as she ended the call. The elevator shuddered as it slowed. She drew in a measured breath, then another. Control first. Always control.

"No one sees you sweat," she murmured, more reminder than reassurance.

The doors opened.

She stepped into the lobby, heels striking marble in steady, deliberate rhythm. Glass walls reflected her back at herself. Composed. Polished. Still dangerous. But the glint in her eyes had dulled, just slightly.

She stopped long enough to really look.

For the first time since Mrs. Lila Mae's death, something unsettled her plans. Not fear. Not doubt. Recognition. She had underestimated the old woman.

She had assumed Country Acres would fold. That the land would bend. That men like Q and Mike would fracture under pressure the way others always had.

She had been wrong.

The realization was small, but sharp. The kind that cuts deeper the longer you pretend it does not exist.

She straightened her shoulders and turned toward the exit. Whatever this had become, it was no longer simple. And it would not be handled gently.

Country Acres had not beaten her.

But it had earned her full attention.

CHAPTER ELEVEN
Land Don't Wait

The work had begun, so the sun made up its mind to rise. Q was already on his feet while the sky still hovered between night and morning, boots planted in the dirt like he'd never left it. He learned early in life that work comes before light.

He checked fence lines by feel, not sight, running his hand along old posts like he was greeting something alive.

For a brief second, his palm paused against one of the tree trunks. The bark was rough. Familiar. The same tree he'd climbed as a boy.

Now there was blood somewhere in its roots.

He didn't flinch.

He didn't apologize.

But he did close his eyes for half a breath.

"You guarded what was yours," he whispered beneath it, not to the tree.

Not to God.

Just to himself.

Then he kept moving.

Mike came out of the house rubbing sleep from his eyes, pulling on a jacket that still smelled like smoke and dew. He stopped for a second, just watching Q work. No rush. No wasted motion. Like the land was speaking and Q already knew the language.

"You always start this early?" Mike asked.

Q didn't look up. "Land don't wait on nobody."

Mike nodded and stepped into it. He grabbed a rake. Then another. He worked clumsy but willing, learning the land one pull at a time. Q noticed. He didn't say a word.

They worked side by side for a while without talking. The sound of metal on dirt. Birds waking up.

The orchards listening to the tune of roosters and cicadas.

"You remember when Red went undefeated for a whole week at the arcade" Mike said finally.

Q let out a small laugh. "She always did cheat."

"She did not."

"She did," Q said, glancing over. "Just did it quiet."

Mike smiled. Hesitantly, he mustered up the courage to ask, "She dating anybody?"

Q stopped raking.

Slowly, he leaned on the handle and looked at Mike like he had just stepped too close to a line.

That's because he did.

"That ain't non'ya business," he said.

Mike raised his hands. "Whoa Romeo, just asking."

Q shook his head. "Candace is family. Always been. When you start talkin' like that... bout my family, be prepared to deal with what come wit'it."

Mike held his goofy look, then nodded. "Fair enough."

That was the end of it.

***

By the time the sun showed itself, trucks were already there, old men stepping down and young boys hopping out after them carrying coolers, tools, and country pride.

One person had brought a pallet of water. A local company supplied chainsaws and huge dumping bins.

The land didn't look abandoned anymore.

It looked defended.

Q stood where everyone could see him. No long, drawn out speech or nothing. Just instructions.

"Brush over there. Fence line needs clearing. Don't stack nothin' we can't reuse. Take all the metal to the landfill. Plastics goes on the back of Lil Willy's truck."

They moved after every breath he took.

Mike watched it happen. How they listened. How they trusted him. He no longer saw a boy playing King. He saw a man the land had already crowned.

He stepped in, hauling limbs and moving boxes, sweating through his shirt, earning looks that turned from curious to respectful.

At one point in the day, he leaned over to Q with a hint of his own southern twang, "After this, we might 'oughta head down to the pool hall and get us a couple beers."

Q smirked. "Careful now. You start talkin' like that, folk gon' thank you belong here."

Mike wiped the dripping lines of sweat dry and grinned. "It's because I do."

By evening, the land looked totally different. Clean. Open. Ready. People stood around like they had just built something that mattered.

That's because they did.

Q and Mike looked out across it together.

No words. Just alignment.

And for the first time, the orchards felt like it was standing up straight again.

****

On the other side of the woods, the meeting room at City Hall filled slower than usual, like folks were dragging their feet toward something they already knew would hurt. Folding chairs scraped the floor. Papers shuffled.

The mayor sat at the head of the table, jacket off, sleeves rolled. He had the look of a man who had already read the headlines twice and did not like what he saw the first time.

Red sat straight in her chair, hands folded, face calm, eyes scanning the room constantly. To her left sat the fire inspector. To her right, Sheriff Haskins, hat resting on his knee.

Across the room, Dana Cross sat with two Magnolia representatives. Clean black suits. Polished shoes. Faces that did not belong to this room.

The mayor cleared his throat.

"Alrighty," he said. "Let's get to it. We've got fires, we've got a dead man, we've got reporters calling this place a war zone. State reps at the Capital are asking what kind of town I'm running."

His eyes landed on Red.

"President," he said. "Start talking."

Red nodded once. "Yes sir."

She didn't rush.

"The fire on the Lila Mae property was not accidental," she said. "Fire reports confirm the presence of accelerants inconsistent with the stored materials on the land. These accelerants were concentrated, precise, measured, and obtained through means most folks in Country Acres do not have."

Cross leaned forward. "If I may," she said smoothly.

The mayor raised a hand without looking at her. "You'll get your turn, Ms. Cross."

Red continued. "The accelerants used were traced back to a supplier contracted by..." she looked disgusted when she said, "Magnolia, Incorporated."

One of the Magnolia reps shifted in his seat. Cross' smile tightened like a chain.

"The death, sir," Red went on, "occurred during an attempted arson on that same property. Two men trespassed with intent to destroy the orchards. Trail cam footage backed this up."

Cross laughed softly. "That is clearly speculation."

Red turned her head. "No. It is evidence and sworn testimony."

The mayor leaned back. "Sheriff."

All eyes in the room landed on Haskins.

He sat still for a moment longer than necessary, looked directly at Cross, and the room got smaller. The look on her face stayed put. It felt like old favors and secrets.

Then he spoke.

"My deputies arrested one suspect for trespassing," he said. "The other was pronounced dead at the scene."

Cross blurted out "And your deputies just let the shooters go, scotch free?"

Haskins corrected her quickly, "Shooter." then continued, "Yes ma'am. He was protecting private property."

The room stirred.

Cross shook her head and with the hint of a venomous threat, "Sheriff, with respect, I believe you *are* choosing sides."

"I am," he responded. "The law's side."

The Magnolia reps exchanged looks and whispers. Cross stood up. "Let's stick to the facts. The land is contaminated and must be sold. Only the right agencies can bring this town into compliance."

Red stood up. "The facts are exactly what we are discussing," she said. "You just don't like where they're leading."

Cross pointed. "Personal loyalties are clouding your judgment. You signed notices against that land yourself, councilwoman."

Red nodded. "I did. Because the law required it. And because Magnolia forced the issue with contaminated reports they created."

Whispers rolled through the room.

Cross scoffed. "There is no proof of that."

"According to these documents recovered from Mrs. Lila Mae's building," Red's voice sharpened. "There is fifty years of it."

Red pulled a single page from the stack.

"Specifically," she said, holding it up, "a 2011 environmental complaint filed against the Dalton farm five miles east of the Lila Mae property. The complaint cited soil toxicity caused by illegal dumping upstream."

She let the paper rest on the table.

"The upstream parcel listed in that report was owned by Briar Holdings, LLC."

She looked directly at Cross.

"Briar Holdings was dissolved three years later. Its registered agent is the same legal representative currently filing permits for Magnolia's development expansion."

Silence.

The mayor leaned forward.

"You're telling me Magnolia used a shell company to contaminate farmland, then leveraged environmental violation fines against those properties to force sales?"

Red didn't blink.

"I'm telling you that it's documented."

The room went still.

The mayor leaned forward. "Explain."

"Q & Mike—" she corrected herself mid-sentence, "Mr. Richards and Mr. Berry uncovered documents hidden in Mrs. Lila Mae's bible," she said.

Cross laughed outright. "This is absurd."

Red turned it up on her. "Mrs. Lila Mae Berry was this town's first elected councilmember," she said. "Before any of us in this room. Before Magnolia ever learned how to pronounce Country Acres."

The fire inspector cleared his throat. "Those documents in discussion include land seizures, chemical dumping, forced defaults, and shell companies tied back to Magnolia," he said. "I've verified them."

Cross's smile vanished.

"You took bribes, you son-of-a-" she snapped.

The inspector jumped up, flinging files everywhere.

"No ma'am. You offered money. You placed it in my office. I ain't ask for it. It's still right here."

He pulled out the envelope stamped, Magnolia, Inc. Sealed and untampered with.

Cross looked at Haskins. "Sheriff."

Haskins shook his head slowly. "Don't look at me."

Her voice rose. "You are all making a mistake."

Red stepped closer to the table.

"You tried to burn our history," she said. "You poisoned our soil. You tried to pay us off. But you forgot something."

She pointed toward the window, toward the land beyond. "Some things in this town can't be bought."

The mayor stood. "Ms. Cross, you and your associates will step outside."

Cross stared at him with a venomous glare. "You don't have the authority to tell me and my associates to do anything."

"I'm the Mayor and I preside over this hearing" he said. "And you're out of line right now Ms. Cross."

Security moved in.

As Cross and her men were escorted toward the door, she looked back at the councilwoman. "This is nowhere near over. Candace."

Red held her ground. "No," she said. "It's just finally coming to the light. Dana."

The door closed. Silence followed. Then the mayor spoke again.

"We will reconvene without outside interests."

The Sheriff placed his hat back on his head.

The fire inspector gathered his documents from the floor. All the council members sat down and gathered themselves.

Somewhere beyond the walls, Country Acres kept breathing, rooted and alive. For the first time in a long while, nobody in that room doubted who the town belonged to.

***

The hallway was empty.
Dana didn't hurry.

120

She walked the length of it with her phone already in her hand. By the time she reached the stairwell, she was dialing.

"They found Briar," she said when the line picked up. No greeting.

A pause.

"No," she continued. "The inspector didn't flip. He logged it."

She listened.

"Then we go for it."

She stepped into the stairwell, voice lower now.

"Pull the Dalton records. Dissolve anything tied to Briar Holdings that still breathes. And get ahead of it. I want a counterstatement drafted before sunset."

Another pause.

"No," she said. "We're not cooling off. It's time to heat up."

Her voice hardened.

"If they want a fight in the dirt, we'll move it to the state."

She ended the call.

CHAPTER TWELVE
Quiet Ain't Peaceful

The sun crept in slowly over the orchard, light spilling through branches that had seen more trouble in one week than most land saw in a lifetime. Birds moved. Livestock stirred. Everything looked perfect. And yet nothing felt settled.

Q stood off in the distance near a barnyard, arms folded, eyes sweeping the property like a wolf counting sheep. No trucks. No volunteers. Just dew clinging to leaves and tire tracks from the night before pressed into the dirt like scars that hadn't healed.

What a week, he thought to himself.

Mike stepped out of the house a moment later, pulling his jacket tight, stretching like a man who had slept but hadn't rested. He made his way to Q.

"What a beautiful morning," Mike said.

Q nodded once. "That mean the fish bitin'."

They didn't say much after that. Didn't need to. The country taught you when to listen.

Mike headed toward the horse stables to check inventory. Clipboards, tools, paperwork. Just the kind of work to stay busy and keep his thoughts from wandering too far. Q stayed back by the barn, ready to labor.

That's when the car rolled in.

Not loud. Not fast. A clean sedan, paint still shining, tires full of gloss. It stopped just short of the gate like it knew exactly where not to cross.

This time, Q didn't see it. Mike did. He had to.

An outsider stepped out, mid-forties maybe, powder blue pressed shirt, creased khaki pants. No dust on his brown shoes. Looked more like he was stepping into a meeting, not onto dirt that had just survived fire and blood.

A half mile back, parked where the road curved behind the pine line, Dana Cross sat inside a tinted SUV, binoculars steady in her hands. She wasn't watching the land. She was watching Mike.

"Michael Berry?" the man called.

Mike straightened up.

Only one person called him Michael.

She was in heaven.

"It's Mike," he corrected the man.

The man held up his hands, friendly. "Name's Alan Whitmore. Insurance. I oversee a few of the policies your grandmother maintained. I was hoping we could talk for a minute."

Q stepped out of the barn.

He locked on it.

He started to bolt toward them but stopped himself. He didn't like it, but he trusted Mike enough to let him stand on his own feet. For now.

He had crossed a line a couple of nights ago. He would not be the reason Mike crossed one now.

Whitmore walked closer, stopping just outside arm's reach. He smelled like clean soap and expensive cologne. Mike was too familiar with that smell.

"Busy few days for you," Whitmore said. "Loss of your grandmother. Property issues. Media trouble. Murder."

Mike's eyes squinted. "You always keep this close of tabs on a stranger."

Whitmore smiled, unbothered. "Information is my job."

He reached into his jacket and pulled out a thin folder. No rush. No force. "I'm not here about the land," he said. "Not directly."

Mike didn't take the folder.

"What then?"

Whitmore lowered his voice, just enough. "I'm here about you. About what's best for *your* future."

Q stayed watching from a distance.

Whitmore continued, calm as a country Sunday morning. "This situation is going to get ugly before it gets better. Investigations all over the place. Lawsuits. Long nights. You could be tied to this place for years trying to fix it."

Mike felt it. The pressure. The invisible hand.

"There are ways out," Whitmore continued. "Clean ones. Quiet ones. Ways where you don't have to bleed for land you haven't lived on in decades."

Mike finally spoke, voice steady, chest inflated. "Say what you came to say."

Whitmore slid the folder toward Mike, smooth and deliberate, as if a table sat between them. Mike grabbed it and looked inside.

Numbers.

Legal terms.

Options.

Dollar signs.

Inside were structured buyout terms. A release from joint liability. A private indemnity clause shielding him from wrongful death litigation. A number that could clear every debt he'd ever had and still leave him wealthy enough to disappear.

Mike saw his Baltimore skyline in those numbers. Saw clean boardrooms. Quiet elevators. No sirens.

No gunshots in orchards.

"Separate your interests," Whitmore said. "Think about what your grandmother left you. *You!*"

Mike stared at the folder. "And Q?" he asked.

Whitmore's smile didn't change. "Mr. Richards will have to make his own legal choices, I suppose."

That felt like the wrong answer.

That's because it was.

Mike stepped back, heat rising in his bones. "Mr. Whitmore. Are you done?"

Whitmore nodded, unfazed. "For now, until you consider it." He turned and walked back to the car. "Think about it," the door closed and rolled away.

Q was already standing beside Mike. "Who that and what he want?"

Mike didn't look at him yet. His eyes stayed on the dust trail behind the sedan.

"He wanted me. Alone," Mike said finally.

Q didn't answer right away. His eyes dropped to the folder in Mike's hand. He let the silence sit between them for a second too long.

"They always do," he said.

Mike tossed the folder onto the porch steps without opening it. "I knew it was too peaceful and quiet around here," he said.

Q noticed he hadn't opened it. Hadn't even looked. He made a mental note.

"In the country," Q said quietly, "quiet ain't peaceful... it's a warning."

They both watched the road like it might answer them if they spoke to it. Somewhere past the tree line, the sedan turned toward the highway, out of their sight. It didn't make it far before someone else decided that it needed company.

Mr. Whitmore rolled to a stop just outside town, at a gas station folks only used when they had no better choice. One pump still worked. One light buzzed overhead. Inside, the clerk didn't look up from her phone until someone reached the counter.

Whitmore stepped out of the car. He didn't like places like this. Too quiet. Too exposed. But Cross had chosen the meeting spot, and he wasn't about to second-guess her. She pulled in right behind him, leaning out the window with that same dumb, forced smile. She didn't falter.

She stepped out of the car and shut the door behind her, heels pounding the gravel as she closed the distance.

Whitmore opened his mouth to speak.

She shushed him. Whatever leverage he thought he had, was already gone.

She reached into her bag and produced an envelope, thick, clean, untouched and sealed, like they always were. She didn't hand it to him. She let him see it.

"There's confusion right now with those policies," she said. "Confusion makes people say things they should not. It makes towns turn on themselves."

Whitmore glanced toward the road. Then back at the envelope. "I don't work for Magnolia. Never have."

"No," she said gently. "You work for me." She slid the envelope onto the hood of his car.

It didn't make a sound.

Inside the station, the cowbell above the door jingled. An old farmer stepped out with a sack of ice over his shoulder. He filled up an empty cooler on the tailgate of his truck. Not enough to be obvious. Just enough to listen.

She leaned in, lowering her voice. "You get Mike to sign over those policies, and you walk away clean."

Whitmore swallowed. "You are assuming that I have control over that man's decisions. You're mistaken."

The smile stayed. Her eyes did not.

"I'm assuming you want to keep your insurance license," she turned to leave, then paused. "Oh," she added, almost as an afterthought. "Just in case you forgot. You were the one who recommended the concentrated kerosene."

Whitmore stiffened. "I didn't recommend anything. You asked me a question."

"You answered it!" she fired back.

She recomposed herself, voice lower now. "And instructing someone how to commit insurance fraud, especially as an employee, comes with a lot of federal time."

She let that sit.

The cowbell dinged again as the old farmer went back inside the store. His truck idled, gray smoke bursting out the tailpipe waiting for his return.

Cross slid into her car and started the engine, the tires leaving a cloud dust as she disappeared down the road.

She didn't check her mirrors once.

She didn't need to.

She was done being careful.

Whitmore stayed frozen, staring at the envelope he had not dared touch. Inside the store, the farmer adjusted his suspenders on his shoulder, watching the man beyond the dirt-stained glass window. He didn't need to ask questions. He had heard everything. Somewhere deep in his chest, a fire ignited.

Q stopped the buzzing of his phone by answering it, "Q? It's Farmer Johnson," the old farmer's voice came through, scratchy but sharp. "I just saw somethin' down by that gas station out past the county line. That Magnolia lady. She's talkin' to some slick dressin' insurance fella."

Q paused. His thumb hovered over the phone like he could crush it in hesitation. "Talk to me."

"Seems like money involved," the farmer continued, leaning back on his porch swing where he could watch the road. "I don't rightly know the whole story, but he's working for her, Q. You prolly'oughta watch who's sittin' beside you."

A hard line formed across his face, silent and deliberate.

Mike hadn't done a thing, yet the seed of doubt found root. The farmer's words carried the weight of every backroad story, every town meeting, every whispered warning.

Q didn't doubt Mike.

He doubted what pressure could do to a man.

The attack wasn't on the land anymore. It was on the space between them.

"I'll keep an eye out," Q said slowly, voice low, steady. "Thanks for lettin' me know."

"That's what we do in Country Acres," the farmer said. "Just... don't let the money blind *you*, son. Some folk don't care who they gotta drag under to get what they want."

Q hung up and set the phone on the counter. He didn't look at Mike.

Not because he didn't trust him.

More because he did.

The words had done their work.

Doubt was back.
And this time, Q couldn't ignore it.

CHAPTER THIRTEEN
She Had Pictures

The office smelled like old leather and stale cigarette smoke. Sheriff Haskins sat behind his desk, fingers running lightly against the wood, eyes fixed on the computer. Red stepped through the door and took a seat. It was as if they had both known this meeting would come to pass.

"Thanks for coming, Ms. Parks," Haskins said, voice low, steady, but carrying a weight that made her straighten. "I need to talk with you, off the record."

She nodded, sensing the tension before he even looked up.

"There's things I signed off on that I shouldn't have," he began, finally meeting her eyes, running a hand through his hair, then letting it fall to the desk. "Since I got elected, I had some agreements."

Red's mind raced.

"Every time Magnolia filed a complaint... code violations, livestock neglect, environmental flags... my office didn't look too hard. And when farmers couldn't pay the fines, the land went quiet."

Her breath caught. She stayed still, letting him continue.

"I didn't think I could stop it." He leaned back in the chair, eyes dropping to the worn surface of the desk. A long silence hung. "Thought I'd be risking everything."

Red's eyes softened, noticing the hesitation, the weight he carried in those quiet seconds.

"But I've always had respect for Mrs. Berry," he said, voice lowering. "That woman was smarter than anyone in this county, even me."

He shook his head lightly, almost in disbelief.

"She knew I wasn't clean. Never said it outright. Just looked at me like she expected better."

Red swallowed, sensing something deeper now. An acknowledgment that the game had been bigger than just land or politics.

"I didn't interfere because I didn't have to. She did everything she needed to protect her land. By herself!" His fingers tapped lightly on the desk, a rhythm of guilt and relief.

Red's eyes softened, but her posture stiffened. "You're saying Magnolia paid you?"

Haskins let out a humorless chuckle. "Paid and played. Well, they didn't play me. Marsha Cross. She got me good."

He lifted his gaze, and for a moment, his eyes met hers fully, almost pleading for understanding.

"Her mother had me in check before Dana came along."

He let the words hang. The silence thick.

"She taught me a lesson I needed. I stayed in line. But now it's time to do the right thing."

Red straightened slightly, a mix of caution and curiosity in her eyes. "And what does that mean?"

"Well," Haskins said, leaning back, rubbing at his temples, "I'm done lying, Councilwoman."

Haskins rose from behind his desk and walked to the wall where a county map hung, corners curled from years of sun.

He tapped a cluster of shaded parcels.

"They don't want orchards," he said.

His finger slid across another block of land.

"They don't want cattle."

He traced a straight line that cut through three former family farms and ended near the county line.

"They want corridors."

Red stood slowly.

"What kind of corridors?"

Haskins grabbed a red marker and drew over the line already faintly sketched across the map.

"Pipeline."

He moved his hand east.

"Rail spur."

He circled a wide clearing near the highway.

"Distribution hub. Natural gas line ties into the interstate grid. Rail connects to the port two counties south. Data center needs cooling access. That creek runs cold year-round."

He stepped back.

"And once it's cleared, it won't be Country Acres no more."

"So they're not buying land," she said quietly. "They're deleting it."

Silence screamed.

The map didn't look like farmland anymore.

It looked like a blueprint for erasure.

He threw it. She caught it.

Her mind raced through the layers of deceit, the fire at the shed, the kerosene reports, the insurance angles. She even thought about the actions of some of her fellow council members.

She pushed it out, "So, where does your loyalty stand now?"

"For Country Acres," Haskins said simply, voice rooted. "For the land. For the people who voted and trusted me to protect it. For everybody I let down along the way."

Red let out a slow breath. The truth settled heavy, undeniable.

"Then we move carefully. We expose them, but we don't start a war we can't finish. Every step has to be clean. Lawful. Airtight."

Haskins nodded. For the first time, he looked lighter, like saying it out loud had stripped years off his shoulders.

"Thank you, Councilwoman Parks," he said.

She gave a small nod and left the room.

***

Sunday morning came and the town gathered where it always did after a week of sins and hard truths.

New Country Acres Baptist Church.

Cars rolled in, dust kicked up behind them, folks stepped out in pressed clothes. Church doors opened and closed as families filed in. Every pew was taken, no more and no less, as if the church itself had taken headcount.

Q stood at the front door helping the elders step inside. He took coats, offered an arm, smiling at every familiar face. The kind of work he had always done without being asked.

Mike came a few minutes late.

Q saw him through the glass before he ever reached the door.

Rushing. Head down. Still buttoning the top of his dress shirt, tie untied. Slipping in like he hoped the place would forgive him for being behind.

At least he showed up, Q thought.

A slight nod between them.

Mike slid into a pew halfway down, breath catching up to him, eyes lifting to the pulpit. He let the room take him in. The wood benches. The worn hymnals. The hush that felt earned. Church always did that to him. It reminded him of who he was supposed to be.

Q was in the back. He stood with the deacons and the old men, hands folded, shoulders squared, eyes scanning the room like he always had. Protector by nature. Guardian by instinct. Mike noticed it then. Q never sat unless the job was done.

The choir finished their song. The room went quiet.

Reverend Johnathon Brooks stepped forward, hands resting on the pulpit. He didn't smile like he normally would've.

"There's somethin' sittin' on my spirit," he said. "Heavy enough that we need to start on a different path today."

The room stilled.

"I want each of you to grab your neighbor's hand. Let's pray."

Heads bowed. The air tightened. His voice was slow and measured, each word placed carefully. He prayed for truth. For courage. For mercy where it could still be found. By the time he finished, the silence felt deep enough to fall into. A baby whined somewhere near the front, then went quiet again.

The reverend opened his Bible.

"Turn with me to First John, chapter one, verse nine."

Pages rustled.

He read it steady.

"If we confess our sins, He is faithful and just to forgive us our sins, and to cleanse us from all unrighteousness."

The words were heavy. Not loud. Not dramatic. Just true.

The reverend closed the Bible.

"This verse ain't about shame," he said. "It's about release. It's about stoppin' the rot 'fore it spreads."

He paused, eyes moving across the room.

"I was contacted this week by someone who asked to speak before this congregation."

A few whispers rippled.

"This person asked for no protection. No favors. Just a chance to tell his truth."

Q felt it before he saw it. A shift in the room.

The reverend stepped aside.

"Mr. Haskins," he said. "You may come forward."

The man who walked up the aisle was not in a police uniform. Whatever power he usually wore had been left outside.

Sheriff Haskins stood at the front of a full church without a badge, without his hat, without the weight that usually announced him before he ever spoke. His hands rested on the back of the pew in front of him.

"I ain't come up here as Sheriff today," he said. His voice carried farther than he expected. "I came up here as a man who owes this town the truth."

The room shifted. Someone cleared their throat. A phone began to ring and was quickly silenced.

"I sinned," Haskins said. "Against God. Against this town. Against people who trusted me to stand when I sat. To speak when I stayed quiet."

Q caught a flicker in Haskins' eyes, the same one he remembered in his father's office when he'd spoken of hard choices and promises that couldn't be broken.

Haskins swallowed, then went on.

"I violated that trust."

Whispers rolled through the pews like wind through corn fields.

"I betrayed Country Acres."

That did it.

Chairs creaked. Someone stated his name like it was a question. Another voice said it like a warning.

Haskins lifted one hand. Not to stop them. Just to steady himself.

"The night I got elected," he said, "I made a stupid choice. I wrecked a patrol car my first week in office. Drunk."

He paused. Let it sit on them.

"Marsha Cross saw me. Or maybe she already knew I'd be there. She had pictures."

He looked up, hoping to gain more strength.

"Said she'd send them to every paper from here to Alaska. Said I'd be finished before I ever got started."

The room went still.

"She told me to ignore some things. Fires. Vandalism. Crops ruined and written off as bad luck. I told myself it was temporary. I told myself I was protecting my family."

His voice cracked but he did not stop.

"Then the envelopes started comin' in. Cash. Quiet. Clean. And every time I took one, it got easier to look away."

A man stood halfway up. "Is that why my cattle got sick last summer."

Another voice followed. "My sheep were killed. I lost plenty of my herd."

"My corn field burnt clean to dirt bout four years back," another said.

"All that spray paint on them buildings that one time," the oldest woman said, meant only for her daughters to hear.

The noise got loud fast. Hurt stacked on hurt.

Reverend Brooks stepped forward, palm raised. "Church," he said calmly. "This is still the Lord's house."

The room settled. Not calm. Just quieter.

Haskins took the mic again.

"I know more people been paid," he said. "I know it in my bones. But I won't name who I can't prove. I already done enough damage with silence."

A woman near the aisle spoke up. "What about the old church?"

Uh oh...

The air changed then.

Country Acres Baptist Church had burned to the ground about 10 years prior. Everybody remembered where they were that night.

Bodies were found in the ashes.

Haskins looked down.

The room waited.

He stopped. Just long enough for the memory to surface.

"That church didn't burn itself."

Reverend Brooks chair scraped hard against the floor. But he stayed in his seat. Attentive.

A familiar face stood. He wasn't in uniform this time around, either.

The fire inspector spoke.

"I was threatened," he said. "And I was paid. Not enough to burn a church. Enough to look the other way."

The truth landed heavy.

Haskins sucked in his breath like it hurt.

"I'm asking for forgiveness," he said. "Not because I deserve it. But because I can't carry this alone no more."

He straightened himself upright.

"I won't be running for sheriff in the next election."

He walked back down the aisle to his seat.

The silence was different. Heavier.

The reverend stepped back to the pulpit.

"This is what confession looks like," he said. "And this is where forgiveness starts. Not with forgetting. With truth."

He bowed his head.

"Search your hearts."

Q stood at the back with the other men, hands clasped in front of him. The words had done their work. Too much truth laid bare. Too many doors opened all at once.

Trust felt thinner than it had an hour ago.

And Q didn't yet know who deserved it.

He looked across the church and found Mike, sitting still, eyes forward. Watching and measuring.

Before the final hymn finished, Red's phone buzzed in her coat pocket. Once. Then again. Then a third time. She didn't look at it. Not yet. But she already knew what it would be.

By the time the congregation spilled into the parking lot, the messages had stacked up. Legal notices. Meeting requests. One voicemail marked urgent from a Magnolia firm out of Atlanta.

They weren't confessing.

They were mobilizing.

And this time, they wouldn't hide behind smoke.

CHAPTER FOURTEEN
That's Not Him

By mid-morning, the courthouse square looked like it was hosting a parade it hadn't asked for.

People crowded the steps and sidewalks, voices rising and falling in uneasy waves. Anger brushed up against relief, and neither one seemed to know where to settle. Some stared at the courthouse doors like answers might walk back out. Others drifted away fast, as if staying too long might tie their names to something they didn't yet understand.

Q stood off to the side, hands in his pockets.

He wasn't watching the people.

He was watching for what didn't belong.

The cameras came first. Tripods bit into the red dirt like stakes. Microphones with bright foam covers bobbed over shoulders. News vans lined the street where pickup trucks usually idled, their satellite dishes turned toward the sky like the town had suddenly become worth listening to.

Country Acres wasn't used to this.

The last time the square had filled with this energy, it hadn't been for speeches or statements.

It had been for sirens.

For whispers.

For a lake that didn't give back what it took from them. That had been thirty-one years ago. And the town had learned what it meant when strangers started taking notes.

Q pushed the memory down and kept scanning.

The patrol cars weren't county-issued. Their decals were stripped clean, their paint too fresh. The men leaning against them wore suits that hadn't ever known red clay or August heat. They spoke into sleeves and earpieces, eyes sliding over the crowd, never resting long enough to be friendly.

Q caught sight of a deputy he'd known since middle school.

The man looked past him like Q wasn't there.

That was when Q understood the rules had changed.

Red caught Q's arm as he passed.

"They filed three injunctions this morning," she said under her breath. "Emergency restraining orders. Property freezes. They're trying to lock you out of your own land before noon."

Q frowned. "That ain't how law works."

"It is when the right judges wake up to the right phone calls," she said.

A black sedan rolled past the square slow enough for them to see inside. Two men. No plates on the front bumper. The passenger lifted a phone and took a picture.

Red didn't move until the car turned the corner.

"They're not trying to win," she said. "They're trying to make this town forget how to speak."

Inside, the courthouse was buzzing. Reporters lined the hallway, voices clipped, questions already loaded. City council members moved in pairs, whispering and avoiding questions, hands busy with phones that wouldn't stop buzzing.

Magnolia had requested a press appearance. They called it cooperation.

That word just didn't feel right.

Q stood near the back of the hall when Sheriff Haskins arrived. He wasn't surrounded by deputies this time. No escort. No commands. Just the weight of what he'd already said, hanging on.

As Haskins got closer to Q, he deliberately slowed down.

"Walk with me, Q" he said quietly.

They didn't go far. They ducked off down a side corridor most people forgot existed. An area with no cameras, no reporters, no echo of applause, no outrage left behind. A place meant for records and storage and things no one planned to revisit.

Haskins stopped near a blank wall. The silence there felt deliberate.

"What I said at church yesterday," he began, eyes forward, "was true."

Q didn't respond. He looked like he wasn't there to hear anything the sheriff had to say.

"But it wasn't all of it."

That got his attention.

Haskins took a deep breath. "Magnolia never planned to see a courtroom. Not really. They like to drag things out. Exhaust people. Make examples when they need to."

His voice lowered. "They're past that stage now."

Q's eyes caught a reflection in the map's glass and two men appeared where no one would think to look.

"Magnolia doesn't clean up loose ends," Haskins said. "They bury them."

The words landed hard, but the delivery was calm. Controlled. Like a man who had finally stopped pretending this was theoretical.

"What that 'posed to mean, Sheriff?" Q asked.

Haskins turned then, the men locking eyes. There was no plea there. No performance. Just a man with accountability.

"They'll come for whoever they think might talk next," he said. "And right now, that's you."

Q didn't like how easily that choice rolled off the man's tongue.

"I need you to fall back," Haskins said. "They know I've talked. Let them think I'm scared. That I want a deal." He paused. "You don't rush to my defense. You keep your distance. Let them believe what they want."

Through the narrow window at the end of the corridor, Q saw black sedans pulling up alongside the courthouse. Doors opening. Men stepping out who didn't bother to look around.

The sheriff waited, letting Q process.

"This building," Haskins said, almost to himself, "isn't safe anymore."

Q felt it then. No panic. No fear. Just clarity.

Whatever had started with land and pressure had just turned into something else.

Outside, the noise rose again. Cameras flashed. Voices all talking over one another.

Somewhere between the sirens and the silence, Q understood one thing with certainty:

The confession at church wasn't repentance.

It was exposure.

Dana Cross stepped to the front of the City Hall stairs like she had rehearsed it for more than just the crowd in front of her.

The microphones were already waiting. Cameras blinked as if on cue. Behind her, Magnolia's legal team stood in a careful line, dark suits, pale faces, hands folded like mourners at a wake they did not intend to attend but knew it would be photographed.

She waited for the noise to settle.

"My heart is so heavy today," she began, the words chosen as carefully as her posture. Her voice carried just far enough, practiced and calm. "What was meant to be a process of cooperation and accountability has instead turned into violence.”

Reporters leaned in.

She didn’t raise her voice. She softened it.

“No one here wants to be the villain,” she said, hands folded in front of her like she was at a graveside instead of a podium. “But legacy can be a heavy thing to carry. It asks sons to become monuments. It asks friends to become fences.”

Her eyes found Q. “Some people leave so they can breathe.” Then more forceful, “some people stay because they don’t know who they are without the weight.”

Murmurs moved through the crowd.

Not anger. Understanding.

That was the dangerous part.

She took a moment to dig up some fake tears, and then she let the words do the work.

“A Magnolia representative is dead,” she continued, letting the title carry more weight than the name ever could. “Murdered on private land during what should have been a routine inspection. A local groundskeeper, inflamed by rumors and misinformation, chose violence.”

A wave of confusion split through the crowd.

“This tragedy is not isolated,” she said. “City council members accepting cash payments. Insurance policies have been mishandled. Public officials who failed this town when *you all* needed them most.”

A hand shot up. “Are you saying the sheriff and city council knew about this?”

“I am saying,” Cross replied evenly, “that multiple safeguards failed. And when safeguards fail, people get hurt.”

Another reporter pressed her. "Didn't Magnolia contribute to those failures?"

Her expression softened. "Magnolia has always acted in good faith. We raised concerns. We asked questions. We trusted local leaders to do their jobs."

She paused, just long enough.

"They did not!"

Phones were already lit up across Country Acres. Kitchen tables, front porches, break rooms. Screens filled with clips, captions, and half-typed judgments as the town took the statement apart word by word.

Group texts flared to life. Church threads. High school groups on social media. Family chains that never went quiet. Someone called the hearing a shamble. Someone else called it a setup.

Nobody called it the truth.

***

Across town, Mike stood in his living room, the television washing the walls in blue light. He didn't sit. He didn't blink. He recognized the cadence, the careful balance of blame that never quite landed where Magnolia stood. His phone was already in his hand.

He dialed Q.

It rang once.

Twice.

Then went to voicemail.

That scared him more than anything Cross had just said.

He grabbed his keys.

***

Back at the courthouse, the Mayor's motorcade arrived. The reporters turned as one.

"Mayor, is this all true?"

"Were bribes taken? If so, how much?"

"Is Country Acres safe?"

The Mayor lifted his hands. "We're here to get answers," he said. "This is an active investigation, we will not rush to conclusions. I promise the people of Country Acres that justice will be served, and everyone responsible will be held accountable."

Behind the microphones, Dana Cross met the eyes of someone off in the distance and gave a small nod no one else seemed to catch.

Q stood off to the side of the crowd, half-shadowed by a parked cruiser. He hadn't looked away since Cross started speaking. His focus shifted across the square. The way certain men stood too still. The way others moved without reason.

Q's eyes caught on something that didn't belong.

Not the man.

The space around him.

The way the crowd bent without knowing why, like creek water around stones.

Then he saw it.

A man stepped out from the line of onlookers. Not rushed. Not hesitant. His path angled toward the Mayor and the Sheriff as they turned back toward the City Hall doors.

Q's mind replayed Haskins' voice from moments before.

Desperate companies erase witnesses.

As the Mayor and Sheriff crossed paths, his hand slipped inside his coat. His movement was precise. Practiced.

When his hand came back, it held a handgun fitted with an extended magazine and a suppressor.

The kind of weapon meant to turn people into rumors.

He never meant to be seen but Q was already moving.

He flew in the air, tackled the man mid-step, the force carrying them both onto the ground.

Bodies collided.

Bones crunched together.

The weapon flew loose and skidded across stone.

For a split second, Q saw it clearly. If that gun had fired, there would be no more meetings, no more records, no more truth spoken into microphones or written into minutes. Just headlines and silence.

"A gun!" someone screamed.

The sound cracked the crowd open. No one knew who it belonged to. No one knew who in Country Acres it had been meant for.

Dana Cross's voice cut across the noise. Loud. Certain. Ready.

"That's him," she said, pointing. "That's the man who murdered our representative. He was going to kill again."

But the crowd didn't surge toward Q. They leaned back instead, like the truth had pushed them there.

They froze.

These were people who had known him their whole lives, who had grown up on the same dirt he worked.

They had watched him work the land, fix fences, carry the old and protect the young.

Whatever this was, they knew was wrong.

This was bigger than a man on the ground. Bigger than a headline. This was about who would be left standing to tell the story of what almost happened here.

Deputies rushed in. Hands grabbed arms. The man was pulled away.

So was Q, just as fast, just as public.

Sirens wailed. Orders were shouted. The courthouse emptied in waves.

Mike's car screeched to a stop just as the handcuffs clicked shut.

He stepped out too fast, door still swinging behind him.

He saw Q being shoved toward a cruiser.

The other man beside him, head down, face hidden.

For a split second, the courthouse steps blurred into the orchard.

Smoke.

Birds exploding from trees.

A body hitting dirt.

The sound of that shotgun.

Mike's chest tightened.

Not again.

Not like this.

He moved forward, but his legs felt half a beat behind his mind.

"Q—"

That was all he got out before the cruiser door slammed.

Blue lights washed over the courthouse steps, turning stone into something colder than justice.

Cross was still at the podium when the noise shifted.

This wasn't a rush.

It was a walk that Red had mapped out long before the sirens started.

She came around the side of the courthouse, with purpose in her stride and a young clerk half a step behind her holding a small video camera tight against her chest.

The clerk didn't aim at the reporters.

She didn't look at Cross.

Her eyes stayed forward, fixed on the steps.

Red didn't break stride.

"You're arresting the wrong man."

She reached the podium, brushed past Cross, and claimed the microphone like it had been waiting on her.

"This ends right now."

Cross turned, lips parting, ready to reclaim the moment.

Red wasn't about to give it back.

"We have this on camera," Red said. "From signal to strike."

Country talk rolled through the crowd.

"The man with the hoodie had the weapon," she continued. "Not Mr. Richards. We can slow the footage down frame by frame. We can show you the signal that she gave him."

The clerk lifted the camera. The lens found Cross before she put her face back on.

She tried to step toward the podium. Red held her ground.

"This was not a lone act," Red said. "It was part of a pattern."

She spoke like someone reading from a file she had already memorized.

"Fires started. Chemicals placed where they didn't belong. Crops ruined. Livestock lost. All designed to drive down land value and force sales."

Someone in the crowd swore under their breath. Another person started crying. Someone shouted a question.

She ignored it all.

"And we have documents," she said. "Records that trace it back to Magnolia, Incorporated. For decades, signed and dated."

The color drained from Cross' face. She glanced toward her team, then toward the street, calculating an exit.

Sheriff Haskins stepped behind her.

Red didn't look back. She had already placed him there.

"Ms. Dana Cross," Haskins said. "You're under arrest for attempted murder. We'll stack the rest of the charges later."

The words landed harder than any shout.

Across the steps, the back door of a patrol car opened. A deputy, under Haskins' order, crossed the distance, unlocked the cuffs on Q, and helped him out of the patrol car.

Red and Q's eyes met for a brief moment.

She winked.

"This isn't over, Candace," Cross said quietly.

Red leaned in just enough for her to hear. "Oh, I know, Dana."

Cross was guided into the same car Q had just left. She paused before ducking inside, her eyes lingered on the councilwoman like a promise she intended to keep.

The door shut. The car pulled away.

Red didn't celebrate.

"This doesn't end today," she said to Q, quietly. "Arrests don't kill corporations. Lawsuits don't either. They drag this out for years. They bury people in paper until they can't afford to breathe."

Q nodded. "Then we need to learn to breathe different."

Red finally exhaled, the kind of breath you take when a plan survived its first contact with the world.

The crowd stood stunned for half a breath, then began to break apart in clusters, already talking, already deciding what version of the truth to carry through kitchens, front porches, and social media groups.

Country Acres seemed to breathe again.

The doors were open. Voices moved easy through the halls. Papers shuffled. Phones rang. It felt ordinary, as if the city had just shrugged off what almost happened.

Red walked up and stopped in front of Q. She didn't say a word. She stepped forward and wrapped her arms around him. Soft. Firm.

Around them, the square seemed lighter. The tension in the air thinned, like the town itself could finally exhale.

From a distance, Mike saw it and paused. From where he stood, it could've meant something else.

It didn't.

It was not that kind of embrace. It was the kind you gave when the danger passed, and the weight finally loosened. The kind family gave each other when words would have done too much.

Q stepped back first. "How'd you know?" he asked.

Red exhaled. "The Sheriff came to me. He didn't know what day it would happen. Just that it would. I trusted him."

Q nodded slower than usual. He understood that kind of knowing.

Mike walked up. Red gave him a small smile.

"I need to get inside," she said. "Council's about to start."

She turned and headed for the doors.

Just before she disappeared inside, Q hollered out, soft but clear. "Thank you, Candace."

The councilwoman glanced back once. Then she was gone.

Q and Mike stood there for a quick second. Then they turned and walked off together, shoulder to shoulder, not sure if anything was coming next.

The map inside City Hall still had a red line drawn across it. That hadn't been erased.

The square cleared out.

The cameras packed up.

The cars rolled away.

But somewhere far beyond the county line, phones were already ringing.

CHAPTER FIFTEEN
Thirty More Years

When they arrived back at the orchards, Q and Mike noticed a lone truck waiting near the edge of the property. Mr. Whitmore leaned against the hood, hands tucked into his pockets.

He looked smaller now. Humbled.

Q scanned him up and down. Waiting. Measuring the man like a twenty-four-inch gauge.

The man lifted his eyes. He got straight to it.

"Mr. Berry... Mr. Richards... I came to make this right," he said, voice low, almost cowardly.

No excuses.

No stalling.

Mike's brows lifted. "Right, how?"

"I came to apologize," Whitmore said, keeping his eyes on Mike as he answered him.

"What I offered you shouldn't have happened. That Dana Cross was threatening my family. I was scared. I was wrong. I hope you can forgive me."

Q's shoulders eased slightly. The first crack showed. Mike said nothing. He just stayed in place, listening.

The man reached into his truck and pulled out two folders.

"Your grandmother's policies... they are intact. Better than you knew. One was even suppressed, hidden from Magnolia. She set it up this way to make sure the land stayed in the right hands, *both of yours.* If you keep it together, it pays five million each. Bonds. Assets. You still keep all the land. Clean. Legal. No funny business. I just need you both to agree and sign."

Mike glanced at the papers but didn't move.

Whitmore waited. Respectful. Composed.

Q reached first, sliding the pen out of the folder. It wasn't for Mike. Wasn't for Whitmore. Not for the long fight they'd all been through.

He signed for Country Acres.

He signed for Mrs. Lila Mae Berry.

He signed for the promise she made them.

One they earned by standing together.

Mike followed without hesitation. The pen scratched across the paper, and with it, an unspoken trust between them cemented itself once more.

The man closed the folder, carefully, reverently, like it had been a sacred thing all along.

"Checks will be in the mail within thirty days," he said with a breath of relief.

Then he turned and walked back to his truck without another word.

Q and Mike stood there and watched the dust rise. The sun was higher now, hotter too.

Mike broke the moment.

"I'm heading back to Baltimore tomorrow," Mike said, casually. "Got a few things to sort out. But I'll be back in a few weeks."

Q smirked. "I heard that one before, Cityboy. Reckon it's gon' be thirty more years 'fore I see you again."

Mike chuckled, shaking his head. He bent over slightly, nudging Q with a shoulder. "It's five million dollars coming next month. And that is not just music to my ears. It is proof that we did this right. I'm here whether you like it or not."

Q let himself smile.

The dirt was now secured.

The fight was honored.

And for the first time, he wasn't standing alone.

Mike gave a final nod and walked toward his car. Q stayed by the fence, chewing on a long piece of straw watching him go.

*****

The orchards rested. The fences stood whole. The red dirt roads had settled back into themselves. After two weeks of chaos and confusion, Country Acres finally slept that night.

Q didn't.

He sat alone in the glow of Mrs. Lila Mae's computer screen, straw tucked at the corner of his mouth, boots still dusty.

He typed the name without rushing it.

MAGNOLIA, INC.

Search results filled the screen.

Permits. Complaints. Shell companies. Quiet acquisitions.

He clicked one.

A zoning dispute from twelve years ago.

He clicked another. A code enforcement escalation tied to a livestock death. Then something older surfaced. A public church fire report.

He clicked the file.

Status: Closed.

Cause: Undetermined.

File Access: Restricted.

Q leaned forward. He noticed something. Three months after the fire, the land transferred. He leaned even closer.

Transferred to a private trust.

Trustee: Lila Mae Berry.

The straw slipped from his mouth.

She hadn't sold. She hadn't walked away, she had acquired. No public statement. No council vote. No ceremony. Just a signature. The purchase had been completed in cash. No lender listed. No delay. No noise.

The trust dissolved seven years later.

Beneficiary: Country Acres Community Fund.

He scrolled further.

Another article from the police department.

Drowning investigation.

A minor.

One adult witness statement sealed.

The year stamped at the top made his eyes open up. He knew that year.

It was the year before Mike arrived in Country Acres. He stared at the screen, looking at the numbers longer than he meant to.

He remembered the heat. The shouting. The yellow tape at the lake entrance. The water going still. A mother screaming her son's name.

The fight hadn't started with him.

It hadn't even started with Magnolia.

It had started with erasing.

Land.

Names.

Stories.

History!

He reached over and pulled Mrs. Lila Mae's Bible closer, resting his hand on the worn leather.

"You been fighting this whole time," he whispered.

He wasn't angry. He wasn't surprised. Now, he was certain.

Outside, the wind shifted through the orchard as the trees rustled.

For the first time, Q understood his half of his inheritance. It wasn't just land, it was unfinished business.

He sat back slowly. Calculating. Not confused. Not betrayed. Measuring and thinking.

He realized that Mrs. Lila Mae had been playing chess. And he had just discovered the board. The more he read, the clearer it became. Magnolia was not the beginning. The church fire was not the beginning.

Whatever was happening in Country Acres had roots that ran deeper than anyone was saying out loud.

The article mentioned an incident from decades ago. Something the town had quietly pushed into the past.

Q clicked on the file attached to the article.

The document opened.

He leaned forward, eyes narrowing as the title appeared across the top of the page.

The Drowning at Junction Lake.